with best wishes

Alexander Martin

Stanley Smartpants
and the Mackerel Robberies

Alexander Martin

Illustrations by Rebecca Clements

First Published in Great Britain in 2008 by
Ambassador Publishing Co.
38 Harris Crescent
Needingworth
Cambridgeshire
PE27 4TE

A CIP Catalogue of this book is available from
the British Library

ISBN 978-0-9560758-0-2

Illustrated by Rebecca Clements

Designed and typeset by
Chandler Book Design

Printed and bound in
Great Britain by
Ashford Colour Press

For Jane

Author's Note

The fictional town of Cat-Haven-on-Sea is loosely based on Paignton in South Devon, and the town of Catmel-by-the-Sea on Carmel in California, USA.

I was inspired to write this story after reading to my two grandchildren, Jack and Katie, who were then 4 & 3 years old – they are now only just 7 and 6. I set out to write a story for them, but it soon turned into a full length novel for older children and intelligent adults!

The Legend of the Birman Cat ......
also known as the Sacred Cat of Burma

The legend has it that priests in northern Burma and Southern Tibet kept these cats as temple companions. The temple of Lao-Tsun, set in a beautiful valley surrounded by mountains, was guarded by 100 yellow-eyed white cats. One day it was attacked by their hated enemies from Siam, and the high priest was murdered. As he lay on his deathbed, his faithful cat, Sinh, gave him comfort. And as his master drew his last breath, Sinh gazed upon the sacred, golden goddess. Sinh was transformed into the most beautiful cat. His eyes became saphire blue to match the eyes of the goddess. His white fur took on a golden glow, and his ears, face, tail and legs became a velvety brown colour. Only the tips of his paws remained white. The other 99 white cats in the temple were similarly transformed the following day.

The Birman Cat Club

Like to see some beautiful Birmans? Then go to the Birman Cat Club website at www.birmancatclub.co.uk and choose Colour Gallery. **WARNING!** If you go to this website and view these beautiful cats, you will fall in love with Birman Cats for ever and ever and ever ..... and you'll just have to have one - or even two!

Acknowledgements

With special thanks to the following, who in one way or another made a significant contribution to the final manuscript: Jane Harman, Deborah Church, Nick Harman, Julie Godfrey.

My thanks also to the incredibly talented Becky Clements, who spent so much time and lavished so much love on producing her wonderful illustrations, which have given extra depth to so many of my characters. Also to Anne Noll who advised me on all things American, to Peter Morris, who photographed the illustrations for design and website purposes, to John Chandler, who designed the book cover and arranged the pdf layout for printing, to Tim Marrow, the mastermind and creator of the Stanley Smartpants website, and to Liza Wilson who devoted a great deal of time towards the development of Stanley's T-Shirts and Fridge Magnets for the website. Also to Joe Fearnley and his colleagues at Ashford Colour Press.

Prior to publication eight children read this story in full. In no particular order they are: Orli Vogt-Vincent, Kiran Datta, Ella Collier, Sophie Pickering, Megan Coulson, Betsy McMahon, Alefyah Anderson, Emily Williams. I asked them to make notes on the manuscript, which were extremely helpful and many of which I was able to use in the final editing process. They also wrote short reviews, all or parts of which are reproduced on the following pages. Apart from the fact that I wanted to write a "good detective story" my main aim was to make my readers laugh. In both regards the comments of the above were most encouraging, indeed heartwarming. Thank you all.

Stanley could only ever have been a Birman, and naturally enough I would like to thank my two Birman cats, Topaz and Rubyn. You can meet them on our website at www.stanleysmartpants.co.uk

Finally I would like to extend my warmest thanks and love to my daughter Jane, who has been a constant champion of my writing, and to whom this book is dedicated.

This book is different from any book I have ever read - in a fantastic way! It has its own unique style, which makes it really fun and exciting to read! I really found this book brilliant! My favourite bits were - well everything and it was hilariously funny! Wrapped with hidden suprises! ~~you don't know~~ keeps you in suspense till the very end, this book I couldn't put down. Instead of humans, there are cats, who are just like us, it's a really good book, because it's out of this world!

For avid readers everywhere, who just love a good book, or want a challenge. Or even a nose for mischef!

Orli-Vogt-Vincent,
age 9, Finchley, London

"I adored Stanley Smartpants,
it is one of the best books I ever read!"

Orli by email

At the end of the story my original text mentioned a game of "pin the tail on the donkey". Orli wrote on the manuscript "it would be funny if it said pin the tail on the mackerel". I thought that was brilliant and asked her permission to use it.

Thanks Orli.

Stanley Smartpants and the Mackerel Robberies

I really enjoyed this book. As Stanley would say "It's soooo cool"!

The story line kept changing and that kept my mind buzzing. It's a great mystery story and has lots of fun humour. I loved the way you made the jokes fit in with the storyline and the character's personalities. I liked Stanleys poems, they were very interesting and clever. I thought changing things into cat version was brilliant, it reminded me that it was a story about cats - on occasion, I found myself forgetting.

It would be nice to have some illustrations, not many but one at the start or end of each chapter?

Thanks for the loan of the book. It was great - I loved reading it. It will go down a storm. Hope all goes well and I look forward to seeing your next book?!

Sophie ☺

Sophie Pickering,
age 11, Cambridge

Book Review - Stanley Smartpants and the mackerel robberies

The book is brilliant.
Once you've started to read t you'll never want to put t down. My favourte thing about the book was that everything had been changed to show that they have been living in a cat's world. Eg. Catdonalds, ktty Kat ice cream parlour, cat diamonds R'us and so on.

Alefyah Anderson,
age 9, Paignton, South Devon

Very, Very funny and a very cool ending

This book is perfect for my age group, and is really funny.

Megan Coulson, 11

Megan Coulson,
age 11, Cambridge

Detective Sergeant Stanley Smart-pants is the cleverest cat in the Cat-haven police force. He and his cat colleagues manage to solve the mystery of the Mackerel Robberies. This story is the funniest book I have read in ages! (And I read a lot!) I found myself laughing so much that my big sister had to read it as well! And believe it or not she laughed and laughed! I can't wait to read the next of Stanley's adventures! Kiran Datta 9

Kiran Datta,
age 9, Finchley, London

I thought that the book was very funny and exciting; my favorite bit was at the end when they played pin the tail on the mackerel. I thought that fitted in well because it is called the mackerel robberies.

I would recommend this book to kids who like cops and action aged around 7-11.

I think the way he transferred everything from human to cat was really clever.

By Betsy McMahon

Betsy McMahon,
age 9, Paignton, South Devon

"I think that it is a very good story opening because right at the beginning he has introduced the main character. I like the way he has used alliteration with all the names .... I like the poems that Stanley Smartpants makes up and I like the way it's always a surprise to see what is going to happen next."

Ella Collier,
age 8, Finchley, London

This book is excellent. I feel it's a mind peeling book I really enjoyed it. The most clever thing that the author did that I loved was that he used places around our town and shops that children love e.g. Toys R. Us changed to Cats R Us. It's very clever and that's one of the things that made me never want to put the book down.

I would recommend this book to someone that's into mysteries and action and likes to have a lot of fun.

Remember this book is not only for boys it is for both boys and girls

Emily Williams
Age 9

Emily Williams,
age 9, Paignton, South Devon

Introduction

Most cats who lived in the town of Cat-Haven-on-Sea hated the stupid names their human owners had given them: names like Snowy, Blackie, Ginger, Whiskey and the like. And once they had escaped from their human homes, gained their independence, and found the thriving cat community of Cat-Haven-on-Sea, their lives had completely changed. No more awful food out of packets and tins. No more eating on the floor for them! Now they could sit at a table and eat with knives and forks, like the civilized creatures they were. Now they could drink real coffee with their cooked breakfasts, eat fresh food like lamb chops and rump steaks, and enjoy champagne and other fine wines. And along with their new lifestyles, they took new names. These adopted names were usually given to them by their cat-friends. Sometimes they were names that just sounded nice. But mostly they were influenced by a cat's personality or characteristics.

CAST OF CHARACTERS (BREED)

A. CAT-POLICE CATS   In order of appearance

Detective Sergeant Stanley Smartpants *(Blue Tabby Point Birman)*
Our hero and principal detective of the Cat-Haven-on-Sea Cat-Police. Intelligent, handsome and beautifully dressed, he has a fine collection of cool trousers. He writes and recites poems about events that occur in the story, and is loved by all the female cats. Has his own website and blog.

Detective Chief Inspector Derek Dimwit *(moggie)*
A plain black and white moggie. The not very bright boss of the Cat-Haven Cat-Police, he is slow on the uptake and easily offended. Stammers when he's flustered, and frequently makes a fool of himself in front of his staff.

Cat-Constable Jumping Jack *(American Wirehair)*
Young, frisky and enthusiastic, he's always jumping around. His frizzy hair stands up on end as if he's had an electric shock. Loves to tell jokes. Has lots of admirers amongst the female cats.

Cat-Constable Tammy Tickletummy *(Seal Point Siamese)*
A real fussy diva, particularly when it comes to food. Fully aware of her rights in the workplace, she stands

up for herself and complains about anything that upsets her. Likes her tummy tickled, particularly when she is upset.

Cat-Constable Marmalade Marmaduke (Red Tabby Shorthair)
Similar in colour to a jar of Seville Orange marmalade. Always eating toast and marmalade. Sensitive about being a little overweight. Has a great sense of humour and is Jumping Jack's best friend.

Greta the Grumbler (Red Classic Tabby Main Coon)
The cat-police station cook and Stanley's secretary, known as the Chief Assistant to the Assistant Chief. Is always grumbling and feels that she is not appreciated.

Cat-Constable Playful Pamela (Black Smoke & White Cornish Rex)
Enjoys playing games. She has long, graceful legs and loves to dance to Tammy's iPod Shuffle. Tammy's best friend.

Cadet-Cat Vacant Vincent aka Vinnie the Poo (Manx)
Frequently stares into space. Suffers from Manx Syndrome, an unfortunate bowel disorder that afflicts some Manx cats. Constantly has to ask in meetings if he can "go for a poo".

Cadet-Cat Studious Stephen *(Blue Cream &*
White Devon Rex)
Wears wire-framed nose glasses and is always reading
books, currently A History of Egyptian Cat-Pyramids.
He likes to think himself superior to the other cats,
and loves to show off his knowledge.

Francesca Forensicca *(Tonkinese)*
A tall, Mediterranean looking cat. She is an American
forensic scientist of Italian descent on loan from
Catmel-on-Sea Cat-Police in California.

Cadet-Cat Soppy Cynthia *(Red Spotted Tabby*
Munchkin)
The newest cadet-cat on the Cat-Haven Cat-Police
force. Has short legs and a short tail and looks a bit
like a squirrel. Is helpless and makes stupid mistakes.
She adores Jack and likes to try and tickle herself so
she can carry on laughing at his jokes.

Apple Pie Annie *(California Spangled)*
American forensic scientist on loan from Catmel-
on-Sea Cat-Police in California. Loves her apple pie.
Serious prankster and practical joker.

B. OTHER CATS

Ping Pong *(Silver-white Burmilla)*

A beautiful Chinese cat. Former winner of the Cat-Haven table tennis championships, she owns a stall in the Fish Market. Derek Dimwit fancies her.

Granny Garbo *(Seal Mitted Rag Doll)*

Former Hollywood cat-movie star. A great beauty in her youth, she is now old and grey. She has cheap spectacles to help with her fading eyesight. Wears old clothes after giving all her Hollywood dresses to Oxfam-cat. *A victim.*

Diamond Lil *(Selkirk Rex)*

Owner of Cat Diamonds 'R' Us jewellery store, and long time friend of Stanley. *A victim.*

Pretty Peaches *(Australian Mist)*

Sales assistant at Cat Diamonds 'R' Us. A gorgeous peach coloured cat who has just started dating Stanley. They met at the ten pin cat-bowling alley after she had slipped on a banana skin and cannoned into him.

Waiter-cat *(Blue Burmese)*

Works at the Cluck Cluck Chicken Diner.

Larry Cluck Cluck *(Norwegian Forest Cat)*
Fat-cat owner of the greasy Cluck Cluck Chicken Diner. Very fat, like a giant balloon ready to burst, he has one terribly obvious glass eye. Suspected of employing illegal immigrants. *A suspect.*

Gorgeous Gloria *(Turkish Angora)*
A terribly pretty cat and part-time waitress at Chez Les Chats restaurant. A student at Catford University studying Portuguese and Tree Surgery. Her long-term career plan is to be a lumberjack in Brazil. All the male police-cats fancy her, especially Jack.

Fearsome Frenchie *(Havana Brown)*
A French cat. Owner of Chez Les Chats restaurant and former professional boxer. Fought for the cat-heavyweight championship of the world against Tuxedo Tyson, and had a chunk of his right ear bitten off.

Scatty Patty *(La Perm)*
Receptionist at the ice-skating rink. Very forgetful. Can't remember what happened one minute ago.

Skatie Katie *(American Wirehair)*
Jumping Jack's sister. Cat-Olympic ice-skating champion, and skating coach at the skating rink. Fancies Stanley. *A victim.*

Beastly Boris *aka* **Yuri Katakov** *(Russian Blue)*
Russian ice-skating champion and part-time dishwasher-cat. Thought to be an illegal immigrant. *A suspect.*

Miserable Melvin *(Abyssinian)*
Manager of the Cat-Odeon cinema. Always moaning and miserable. *A victim.*

Curious Connie *(Scottish Fold)*
A white cat with red stripes and blotches on her fur after an unfortunate accident in a washing machine at the launderette. Works at the ice-skating rink.

Precious Gemma *(Turkish Angora)*
Sales assistant at Cat Diamonds 'R' Us.

Klepto Klaws *(Sphinx)*
An ugly cat with a black patch over one eye and a wrinkly almost hairless body. Lives in a large detached house near the top of Cat-Haven hill. Suspected of handling stolen goods. *A suspect.*

Wanda *(not specified)*
Waitress at the Sea View Café, who has an argument with Klepto Klaws, and tips up his plate of sausages, beans and chips into his lap.

Sing Song *(Lilac Silver Shaded Burmilla)*
A good looking, smartly dressed cat who meets Klepto Klaws in the Sea View Café. Ping Pong's brother. *A suspect.*

Taxi Driver *(Seal Mitted Blue Snowshoe)*
Jack instructs him to ….. "follow that car".

Lollipop Lola *(Ragamuffin)*
Manageress of the Kitty Kat Ice Cream Parlour, where all kittens are given free lollipops. Wears an incredible cotton dress, printed with pictures of ice cream cones, fruit sundaes, banana splits and knickerbocker glories. Fancies Stanley. *A victim.*

Waitress-cat *(Cornish Rex)*
Waitress at the Kitty Kat Ice Cream Parlour.

Vladimir Katakov *(Russian Blue)*
Russian handycat at the Cat-Odeon cinema. Thought to be the brother of Yuri Katakov. *A suspect.*

Mystery Cat *(Not known)*
Blue-grey or silver blue. Seen hanging around at several of the crime scenes a few days before the robberies. Thought to have a limp. *A suspect.*

Albert Tartpincher *(Blue Burmese)*
Window cleaner at three of the crime scenes. Suspected

of stealing squintillions of jam tarts from the Albert Hall, and arrested over the theft of pineapple tarts from the cat-bakery. *A suspect.*

Spit and Polish *aka* **Laszlo Kiss** *(Blue Burmese)*
Hungarian office cleaner who cleans three of the crime scenes. A musician who plays the hurdy-gurdy at the Magyar Palace Restaurant. *A suspect.*

Billy Blunderhead *(Blue Korat)*
Part-time waiter at the Cluck Cluck Chicken Diner. Terribly clumsy. Falls over his own feet and constantly mixes up food orders. *A suspect.*

Saucy Suzette *(Blue Ocicat)*
French chef at Chez Les Chats restaurant. *A suspect.*

Calculating Calvin *(Russian Blue)*
Book-keeper at Kitty Kat Ice Cream Parlour. *A suspect.*

Ten Bangles Tonia *(Russian Blue)*
Sales assistant at Cat Diamonds 'R' Us. *A suspect.*

Mr Forty Winks *(Asian Smoke)*
Owner of the Feline Furniture Emporium, he has a large stock of comfy chairs and sofas designed for cats to enjoy a comfortable catnap. *A victim.*

Harriet Fishnet *(American Black Bombay)*
Three legged fishercat who fishes for mackerel at sea off Torcat beach. *A victim.*

Cauliflower Colin *(Blue Korat)*
Projectionist at the Cat-Odeon cinema. Eats cauliflower sandwiches. *A suspect.*

Sheriff Chuck Smartpants
(Chocolate Point Birman) Stanley's cousin. Chief of the Catmel-by-the-Sea Cat-Police in California.

Annuska *(Turkish Angora)*
Hungarian cat at the Magyar Palace Restaurant who entertains her fellow diners by dancing wildly on a table.

Vodka Valentina *(Russian Blue)*
Waitress at the Bling Bling Bar and sister of Beastly Boris/Yuri Katakov. Fancies Marmalade Marmaduke, and he fancies her.

Friday 7th July

One summer afternoon, just after lunch, Detective Sergeant Stanley Smartpants of the Cat-Haven Cat-Police was deep in thought. He sat at his office desk, chewing the end of a pencil. He was trying to figure out why any cat would want to leave the bones of a dead mackerel in another cat's house. It was a puzzling mystery.

Stanley was a Blue Tabby Point Birman, and generally regarded as being a very handsome cat indeed. He had a thick coat of creamy-white fur, a bushy, fluffy, brownish tail, and intense sapphire blue eyes. The distinctive brown markings on his beautiful face and his chocolate brown ears were his most interesting feature. But it was the stylish way he dressed that made him stand out from other cats. Today he was dressed in one of his favourite outfits, a pair of red and black striped trousers and a bright blue waistcoat that matched his eyes. He also wore a really cool pink bow tie with large white spots.

The telephone jangled noisily, interrupting his thoughts. It was his boss, Detective Chief Inspector Derek Dimwit. Stanley listened for a few moments. Then he hung up the phone, left his office, and walked across the corridor. Derek's office door was open and Stanley went straight in.

"Now look here, Stan," said Derek, "I told you I didn't want these mackerel bones on my desk."

"I agree. They shouldn't still be here. I'll get them sent down to the lab for examination. This is a fishy business, Chief."

"Very funny, Stan."

Stanley smiled. "Seriously though, I think we should go down to the Fish Market and see if we can find any clues."

Derek Dimwit stared at Stanley in annoyance. "I was just planning to have a little snooze in my office chair."

Stanley Smartpants was renowned in the Cat-Haven Cat-Police force for his ability to think on his feet, and make up a poem to suit every occasion. This was one such occasion:

> "If you want to catch the criminal-cat,
> In your swivel chair you should not be sat.
> Get on your feet,
> Out in the street

Get out there, Chief.
Hunt down the thief!
'Cos if you're out there on the ground,
You'll find the clues that are around.

There's no time for sleeping, Chief, if we're to get to the bottom of this. You should know that, what with you being the boss and all. You spend too much time sleeping. We'll never crack these cases if we spend half our day asleep."

Derek Dimwit checked his mickey-mouse watch. "It's ten to two already," he said accusingly. "It's definitely time for a sleep."

"But your watch always says ten to two. And it has done since the day it was given to you by the owner of that back street jewellery shop."

"That's beside the point," said Derek irritably. "I don't want to go to the Fish Market."

Stanley jumped down from his chair. "Now come on now, Chief. It'll be better than a slap in the eye with a wet fish. And besides, you'll be able to see Ping Pong." He hitched up his trousers and made for the door.

Derek tried to screw up his face in a gesture of disgust, but it didn't really work. His was a face without expression. His coal black, unblinking eyes stared out of a plain, simple black and white face. He was not a pedigree cat. He was a cat of no particular breed. To be blunt, he was just an ordinary moggie.

"All right," he said. "But let's check out what's going on in the Crime Room first."

Stanley opened the door to the Crime Room to be greeted by the sound of the Scissor Cats latest hit, 'I sure do feel like dancing'. Three of the cadet-cats were taking the title of the track literally, and were dancing wildly on the conference table. Cat-Constable Jumping Jack was standing on top of his desk, surrounded by several of the female cadet-cats, all of them laughing out loud. "Hello, Sarge. We're just in the middle of our break. I've been telling a few jokes. How about this one? What's orange and sounds like a parrot?"

Stanley shook his head. "I've no idea."

"It's obvious really. It's a carrot! Ha! Ha! Ha! I thought you'd have got that one, Sarge!" Jack's female admirers laughed some more.

"You cats should be working," said Chief Inspector Dimwit, "instead of jigging around the office."

"It's our official tea break," said Tammy Tickletummy indignantly. "We're entitled to do what we want." Cat-Constable Tammy Tickletummy was a Seal Point Siamese, a slim cat who had a soft, white coat with shades of light brown. She had an impish, pointed face that was dark brown almost black. She glared at her boss defiantly.

"There are m-m-m-m-more important things to be d-d-d-doing." Derek Dimwit had an unfortunate stammer when he was flustered or unsure of himself.

Stanley interrupted. "The Chief and I are going to the Fish Market. Jack, you're in charge while we're gone."

"No problem, Sarge." Jumping Jack leaped down from his desk. He was a young and very frisky cat. His colouring was black and grey in a tabby pattern, and he had a brilliant white neck and a white blaze between his eyes and round his nose and mouth. His hazel green eyes were bright and intelligent, and full of fun. He was an American Wirehair and his frizzy fur stood up on end, as if he'd suffered an electric shock. He was always jumping around, and quite often it got him into trouble. One time he was in the kitchen and jumped up onto the worktop. Unfortunately he landed on top of the electric toaster, while it was on. He sat right down on the red-hot toaster and it frizzled his bum. And it made his hair stand up even more!

"Make sure everyone behaves sensibly, Jack," said Stanley. "I'm relying on you."

Jack grinned. "No problem, Sarge!"

Stanley noted the gleam in Jack's hazel green eyes, but said nothing. Better not to encourage him, he thought.

"Let me open the door for you, Sarge."

"Not trying to get rid of us in a hurry are you, Jack?"

"Who me, Sarge? How could you even think it?"

Incredibly, as Jack opened the office door, a mouse

with a large piece of cheese in his mouth, shot into the room.

"Miaow!" cried Tammy. "I hate mice." She ran towards Marmaduke, jumped into his arms, and clung on.

"Oh, oh," said Jack, "Panic Pants is in a flap!"

Marmaduke dropped the toast and marmalade he had been eating and it fell on the floor. Marmalade side down! Cat-Constable Marmalade Marmaduke was a Red Tabby Shorthair, and his coat was remarkably similar in colour to a jar of orange Seville marmalade. It contrasted nicely with his black trousers. He was a little overweight and had a large, round, fat face, on which sat a broad, snub nose. His huge eyes were a bright olive green.

Jack was also quick to react, and threw his coffee mug at the mouse. He'd forgotten that the mug was still half full of coffee and the sweet, brown liquid splashed onto the wall. A few drops of coffee landed on Derek Dimwit's face, and he licked them off.

"Goodness gracious, you take your tea pretty strong, Jack," he said.

Jack thought about telling the Chief that it was coffee, not tea, but decided not to bother. "Sorry about that, Chief, but it seemed like the best thing to do."

The mouse had come to a dead halt in the middle of the office. The frightened little creature looked around and found himself surrounded by an army of cats. It was a terrifying situation for him. His knees started knocking, and he was trembling from head to tail.

"Leave the poor little creature alone," said Stanley. "He's sooooo cool, and he's not doing us any harm, is he? Chuck, chuck, chuck, chuck ….." he cooed, looking the mouse straight in the eyes. "Come on, little chappie, off you go. We're not going to hurt you. Chuck, chuck, chuck ….. Take your cheese with you now, little fellow."

The mouse was bewildered. It seemed that this very important cat was going to let him go.

"Come on now, take the cheese with you," Stanley murmured, in what he hoped was an encouraging tone of voice. "As long as it isn't our expensive cheese!" He looked in Derek Dimwit's direction. The Chief Inspector was partial to a bit of Blue Stilton with his coffee after lunch.

The mouse finally plucked up courage and moved slowly towards the door. Gradually he increased his speed as he saw that not one of the cats assembled in the office was going to attack him. With a loud squeak of relief he raced through the door to freedom.

Friday 7th July

Cat-Haven-on-Sea was a small seaside town in the county of Devon in the south west of England. The cat-police station was situated opposite the park, not far from the Tesco-Cat supermarket. Stanley and Derek took a panda car from the motor pool and drove into the centre of the town. Stanley was driving, his white paws gripping the steering wheel tightly, his breathtakingly blue eyes alert and watchful.

They passed the level crossing which divided the main shopping area of the town from the sea front. Turning right at the sea front road, they drove with the sea on their left, and almost immediately passed the Cat-Odeon cinema and the 'Crazy Golf for Crazy Cats'. Soon they were at the harbour, chock full of fishing boats bobbing gently on the calm waters of high tide. They parked outside the Fish Market in the area reserved for fishercats and traders.

They entered the market, and stood surveying the scene. There were cats of all shapes, sizes and colours, scurrying back and forth, many of them carrying trays of fresh fish on their heads. In the centre of the market was a stall selling tasty fishy treats. Stanley stopped to buy sardines on toast in small bite-size pieces. Derek bought himself a crab sandwich on crusty brown bread.

After polishing off their tasty treats, the two cat-police made their way towards the far side of the market. The wonderful smells of sea and fish were in their nostrils, and the flavours of sardine and crab were on their lips. They were looking for the beautiful Chinese cat known as Ping Pong.

Ping Pong's given name was Hing Hong, but when in the same month she won the Cat-Haven-on-Sea table tennis championships and took a stall in the Fish Market, she acquired the name of Ping Pong.

The two cat-police had to push through a throng of cats milling around in the gangway. Ping Pong spotted them straightaway. She was a silver-white Burmilla, shaded in brown, with lustrous green eyes. She flashed a brilliant smile at Derek, who blushed ever so slightly. It was common knowledge amongst the cat-citizens of Cat-Haven-on-Sea that the Chief of the Cat-Police fancied Ping Pong.

"We're investigating the mysterious death of a mackerel, Ping Pong, and wondered if you might be able to help us," said Derek.

"You know I'll help in any way I can, Doody." Ping Pong smiled brightly, and brushed imaginary dandruff from his collar. Derek seemed to cringe, perhaps embarrassed at Ping Pong's use of a special nickname.

"I know you sell squintillions of fish, Ping Pong," said Stanley, "and it may be difficult to remember, but have you sold much mackerel this week?"

"Now let me see ...." said Ping Pong struggling to remember.

"What does squintillions mean, Stan?" said Derek.

"It's great isn't it? It's my new word, it means loads and loads ..... *squintillions* of fish ......" Stanley stressed the word squintillions heavily .... "It's soooo cool isn't it?

"Yes, I like it Stan. It's a good word."

"Was the dead mackerel fresh then?" said Ping Pong.

"It's difficult to say at the moment. We haven't had the forensic report."

"What's a forensic report?"

"Well, in this case the forensic cats examine the dead mackerel in order to discover the cause of death. In other situations they examine clues like pawprints, articles of clothing, cat hairs and so on, so that we can prove who the criminal-cat is. That's forensics, and it's a vital tool in our work to solve crimes, Ping Pong. Anyway, back to your mackerel sales."

"I bought a large quantity from Harriet Fishnet, the three-legged fishercat. I sold quite a few to individual customers, but I sold most of them to Fearsome Frenchie for his restaurant. Oddly I also sold some to the owner of that fast food place, the Cluck Cluck Chicken Takeaway."

"Not as odd as you might think," said Stanley. "I went in to the Cluck Cluck Chicken one day last week to pick up a snack. I had a really cool chickenburger and chips." He licked his lips at the memory. "Anyway, while I was waiting for the food to arrive I discovered that they've opened up a new diner at the back, and according to the menu there were several fish dishes. I think I'll go and have a meal there later. You never know what might turn up. Thanks for your help, Ping Pong."

"Are we going back to the station now, Stan?" asked Derek hopefully.

"I think we ought to visit the old lady-cat, Chief."

"You mean where the skeleton of the dead mackerel was found?"

Friday 7th July

They followed the coast road, past the cat-casino where Stanley Smartpants had not been very smart one night and had lost his shirt and his trousers, gambling on the spin of the roulette wheel. And on past The Cat and Fiddle pub, where only a week ago he had arrested a black tomcat for pouring a glass of beer over his companion. They were arguing about whether or not Catchester United should have been awarded a penalty in last Sunday's televised football match against the Cat-Haven Gooners.

Stanley had not been in the cat-police force all his working life. As a young cat he had been a professional footballer, playing for the Cat-Haven Gooners. He was their star striker and had been selected to captain England's Cat-World Cup squad. Sadly, only a matter of weeks before the team was due to travel, he broke a metatarsal bone in his foot, and had to withdraw from the squad. Despite the attention of the best surgeon-cats in the country, the injury had never healed properly, and he was forced to retire. It was the influence of his cousin Chuck, who was in the cat-police force in California, that prompted him to join the Cat-Haven cat-police. And in truth, he preferred detective work to playing football. It was much more challenging. Derek Dimwit on the other hand, had joined the cat-police force straight from school, after failing all his exams. However, he had worked hard in those early years, and finally got his reward when his cousin, the Mayor, had appointed him as the Chief of the Cat-Haven Cat-Police.

Stanley checked his rear view mirror. What he saw startled him. A motorbike was closing in fast. It raced past them. A large male cat in black leathers and a yellow helmet was driving, waving his paws around like a windmill. He was showing off to his girlfriend-cat, who was clinging on to his waist. She nearly fell off as the motorbike swerved to pass the panda car.

"They must be travelling at twice the speed limit," said Derek. "Not to mention driving dangerously. We ought to pull them in, Stan."

"You're right, we'll have to deal with it. Put in a call to the office, Chief, and I'll speak to Charlie."

Derek rang the office on the hands free. The

phone was answered after two rings. "Hello, Cat-Haven Cat-Police. Cheerful Charlie speaking. How can I help you?"

"Charlie, it's me," said Stanley into the microphone. "We're on the coast road going towards Brixcat. We've just passed the Cat and Fiddle. There's a lunatic cat driving a motorbike. He's just screamed past us at twice the speed limit. I'm pretty sure he's on an Extreme Yellow Yamaha Super Sport Y2F-R1. It's a massive beast. Can you check if there's a car up ahead that could intercept him."

"You're pretty clued-up on bikes," said Derek.

"Yeah, when I was young I went motorbike scrambling squintillions of times. I still keep up with the latest models. That's an expensive bike, Derek."

"I really do like that word, squintillions. Can I use it, Stan?"

"Of course you can, Chief."

"You're in luck, Stan," said Charlie over the radio. "Jack and Marmaduke are on the coast road right now, on the way back from Brixcat. I'll get on to them right away."

"Thanks, Charlie. That's a big help to us."

Almost on the edge of town they came to a row of terraced houses, where Granny Garbo lived. Stanley knocked at her door. It took a while before she opened it. She had been a Hollywood cat-movie star many years ago, but she was old now. She was a Seal Mitted

Ragdoll, her once white fur now grey, but her face was beautiful still, and her blue eyes still captivating. It was easy to appreciate that she had been a great beauty in her youth, but none of that mattered to her now. She had arthritis in her joints, and she wore cheap spectacles to help with her fading eyesight. She was wearing old clothes because she'd given all her Hollywood dresses to Oxfam-cat, the cat-charity shop in the centre of town. She peered at them suspiciously. "Yes, who are you?"

"Hello Granny Garbo, we're the cat-police. I'm Detective Sergeant Smartpants, and this is my colleague, Detective Chief Inspector Dimwit."

"I suppose you're here about the dead mackerel."

"May we come in?" said Stanley.

Granny Garbo said nothing, but turned her back on them and hobbled uncomfortably towards the back of the house. The two cat-police officers followed her into the kitchen. There was a wonderful smell of freshly baked bread, and there on the kitchen table stood a bowl of steaming hot tomato soup. Stanley immediately felt hungry and when he looked at Derek he could see from the expression on his face that he too was hungry. Fortunately their training in the cat-police force took over, and although it was an extreme effort of self-control, they stopped themselves from jumping onto the table to scoff Granny's soup.

"First of all Granny," said Stanley, "can I confirm that the mackerel wasn't yours?"

"That's right," squeaked Granny.

"Where did you find it?"

"It was upstairs, in my bedroom."

"Perhaps the criminal-cat stole it from Granny's fridge, ate it in the kitchen, and then took it upstairs," suggested Dimwit.

"It wasn't Granny's mackerel, Chief."

"Oh, yeah."

"I suspect," said Stanley thinking out loud, "that the criminal-cat brought it into the house, then took it upstairs to eat. Hmm. Were there any signs of forced entry, Granny?"

"If you mean was the door broken down, or a window smashed, the answer's no."

"Could any cat have jumped through an open window?"

"No. At my age I feel the cold, so I always keep the windows shut. If it's really hot, I've got air conditioning, so I don't need to open the windows anyway."

"Does any other cat have a key to your house, Granny? Relatives, neighbours?"

"I keep myself to myself. I prefer it that way."

"Have you had any visitors in the last few days? Tradescats perhaps? Any deliveries?"

"No, nobody."

"Has anything gone missing?"

"No."

"Have you checked thoroughly, Granny?"

"There's nothing to check."

"OK, you'd better show us where it was found."

"I was just about to eat my soup," grumbled Granny Garbo. "Can't you come back later?"

"Granny, cat-police time is precious," said Derek, trying to be a clever dick, "as I'm sure you'll appreciate. Anyway it'll give your soup a chance to cool down, so you won't burn your mouth."

Granny gave the two cat-police officers a dirty look, and reluctantly hobbled out of the kitchen. They climbed the stairs in silence.

"It was right here," she said, pointing to a spot in front of the dressing table.

"Which way was the head facing?" said Dimwit rather pointlessly.

"What's more important," said Stanley, "is did he leave a clue?" They began to search the room. "Ah!" he exclaimed within moments. "What's this?" There was a clear print of a cat's paw on the left hand edge of the dressing table. He took a small piece of chalk out of his waistcoat pocket and drew a circle round the pawprint. They continued with their search but found nothing else of interest.

"I'd be grateful if you wouldn't clean anything in this room until our forensic cats have been, Granny," said Stanley. "I'll send them in later this afternoon to lift the pawprint and check things over, see if there is anything that we've missed."

Granny looked relieved. "Can I get back to my tomato soup now?"

As they left Granny's house the rain was streaming down. They saw a tabby cat walking briskly along the street, sheltering under a large blue and white golf umbrella. Derek Dimwit was so busy looking at the cat with the umbrella that he failed to see a large puddle of muddy water, and stepped straight into it. His once shiny black shoes were now covered in dirty brown mud.

"Dear, oh dear!" said Stanley.

"It's worse than dear oh dear. Look at my shoes? They're ruined."

"They'll soon clean up, Chief. It's better than a slap in the eye with a wet fish."

"Huh! Anyway, never mind that. Granny Garbo's turned out to be a waste of time, didn't it?"

"I'm not so sure about that. It seems to me that the criminal-cat, if that's what he is, knows Granny. Or at least he knows how to get into her house without her realising it."

"I hear what you say, Stan, but I don't get it. What do you mean *if* he's a criminal-cat?"

"We haven't established that he did anything wrong, apart from gaining entry to Granny's house. She may have forgotten about a visitor she's had. She *is* old, you know, despite her looks. Why would the skeleton of a dead mackerel suddenly turn up in her bedroom? It doesn't make any sense. We're definitely missing something here, Chief."

****

Before they reached the car Stanley's mobile phone rang.

"There's been a robbery," said Cheerful Charlie. "At the Cat-Diamonds "R" Us jewellery store in the High Street."

Friday 7th July

Their car came to a halt on the double yellow lines outside Cat-Diamonds "R" Us. They strode into the shop and were greeted by the owner-cat, Diamond Lil. "Thank goodness it's you, Stanley," she said. "Somebody robbed the till while we weren't looking."

"Hello, Lil, it's good to see you again," said Stanley.

Diamond Lil smiled, and lowered her head to lick her glossy black fur. She was a black smoke Selkirk Rex, with a curly black coat and large, round, copper-coloured eyes.

"Oh, this is Chief Inspector Dimwit, by the way." Stanley probed gently. "What's been stolen?"

"There's some money missing from the till, but we're not sure how much."

"A rough idea?"

"A couple of hundred cat-euros I should think. I'll be able to let you know exactly when I've balanced the cash."

"When did you discover the loss?"

"Less than an hour ago. I rang the cat-police station more or less straightaway. I'm surprised that you got here so quickly."

"Who actually discovered the loss?"

"I did. I'd just served a customer-cat, and went to the till for change."

"What about jewellery?"

"I don't think so."

"Any clues?"

"I don't know if it's a clue or not, but we found some mackerel bones over there." She pointed to the floor, underneath the counter where the till was.

"Goodness gracious!" exclaimed Derek. "Another dead mackerel! Do you think it's a coincidence, Stan?"

"I doubt it, Chief. Has the mackerel been moved, Lil?"

"No, I found it myself, and told everyone not to touch it. I thought it might be important."

"Good girl."

"If it's not a coincidence, Stan," said Derek, "do you think the criminal-cat is the same one who broke in to Granny Garbo's house?"

Sergeant Smartpants lowered his voice so that none of the other cats in the shop would overhear him.

"I have mentioned this before, Chief, it really isn't a good idea to discuss confidential cat-police information in front of the cat-public."

Suddenly there was an ear-piercing scream from the other side of the shop. "Miaooooow!"

Diamond Lil looked in the direction of the scream, and her black face turned white with shock. It was one of her shop assistants, Pretty Peaches, a gorgeous peach coloured cat, and she was holding up an empty jewellery display tray. "Oh no!" cried Diamond Lil. "That's the cabinet where we keep our best jewellery!" She rushed over to Pretty Peaches, closely followed by Stanley and Derek. "Let me see." She snatched the empty tray from Peaches' paws. "Oh no!" she cried again, wringing her paws in anguish, "This is a disaster. Our most expensive diamond necklace has gone! It's worth ten thousand cat-euros!" Huge cat-tears fell out of her eyes in a flood, and rolled down her beautiful cheeks. "Oh, Stanley, how could this have happened?"

Stanley put two comforting paws round her waist and held her tight. "We'll find the criminal-cat, Lil, I give you my word. And we'll get your necklace back." With difficulty he detached himself from Lil's clinging embrace.

"Hello again, Peaches," he said. "Its nice to see you. Pity the circumstances weren't different."

Peaches smiled. "It's good to see you too, Stanley."

"You two know each other then?" said Lil.

"Yes we met at the ten pin cat-bowling alley last week. We sort of fell over each other. It was sooooo cool!" Stanley grinned at the memory. He had been about to launch a ball down the lane, when Peaches had come flying into him. She had slipped on a banana skin that shouldn't have been there. They fell into a heap, Peaches all apologies, Stanley all smiles. Actually he couldn't believe his luck! He had spotted Peaches earlier in the evening and was wondering how he might approach her. When she literally fell into his lap it was a simple matter to invite her out for a drink. They had been to the Cat and Fiddle two nights ago.

"As a matter of fact," said Stanley a little sheepishly, "I've written a poem about it ….. if you'd like to hear it?"

"Oh yes," said Peaches excitedly.

"OK, here goes …….

I jumped up to bowl, and I took a big leap.
But before I could throw I fell in a heap.
Once on my feet I did hitch up my breeches.
And who did I see? The beautiful Peaches!"

"Oh, that's wonderful Stanley." Peaches clapped her paws together. "How clever you are!"

"It's good, Stanley," said Lil.

"I'm glad you both like it." Stanley blushed ever so slightly. "Anyway, back to business. I'm sorry, Lil, but

I must ask you to examine the cabinet and tell me if anything else is missing."

"Of course, Stanley." Lil wiped the tears from her eyes with a silk handkerchief. She studied the cabinet, which had more than twenty trays of assorted necklaces and rings. "No," she said after a while. "The only thing that's gone is the diamond necklace. It was the most expensive piece we had in the shop."

"Are you sure, Lil? You've got squintillions of stuff here."

"I'll know when I've done a thorough check, but it looks like it's the only thing missing."

"We'll send in the forensic cats first thing tomorrow morning. In the meantime, I'd appreciate a description of the missing necklace. How many diamonds, that sort of thing."

"Yes, of course, Stanley. I'll look up the details on our cat-computer catalogue. I'll be back in a minute."

While Lil was in the back office Stanley and Derek checked the area around the display case for several minutes.

"Ah!" said Stanley triumphantly, "look what we've got here." He held up a short blue-coloured hair and a small square of heavy grey cotton, which seemed to have been torn from something. "Now we're getting somewhere. This piece of cotton could be from a pair of jeans." He took a small plastic bag out of his waistcoat pocket, together with a pair of tweezers, and carefully deposited the two items in the bag, which he then sealed and put back in his pocket.

"Do you think that piece of cloth was torn from the thief's trousers, Stan?" said Derek.

"It's possible. At least we know that it didn't come from any of the staff."

"I hear what you say, Stan, but how do you know that?"

"Derek, all the staff are female cats, they're all wearing the Cat-Diamonds "R" Us uniform of pink skirts and silver grey blouses. This material seems to be grey denim, perhaps torn from a pair of jeans."

"You're so smart, Stan. Is that why they call you Stanley Smartpants? Or is it because you bought all those fantastic trousers in New York?"

"It was buying those trousers in New York, Chief."

"Why don't they call you Smarttrousers?"

"Americans call trousers pants, Chief."

"I know that," said Derek Dimwit, sounding hurt. "I'm not completely stupid. Anyway, you do seem to have a lot of different 'pants', if that's what you want to call them. I suppose you've got squintillions of them?"

Stanley laughed. "Not exactly, but I have got an awesome collection, Derek. They're soooo cool!" Stanley sounded really excited. "I'm thinking of putting a collection of them on my website, **www.stanleysmartpants.co.uk** ."

"You've got your own website?" said Derek Dimwit incredulously.

"All cool cats have their own website, Chief."

"Well I don't."

"Well …. never mind." Stanley didn't know what else to say.

"What have you got on your website?"

"Loads of exciting stuff! There's the Stanley Smartpants Blog, with all my current news and views. I update it regularly, and anyone can post comments on it. I've got pictures of all my friends and colleagues, even you, Chief."

"Oh, really," said Derek, his curiosity aroused. "Tell me more."

"And there are also examples of my poems, and Jack's jokes. There are competitions and prizes for all my friends around the globe – they can send in special "Stanley style" poems, and cool jokes, and win a prize! They can download a picture of me that they can colour in. And you never know, Chief, if somebody can design a really cool outfit with great trousers, waistcoat, bow tie …. I might even get it specially made for me! And they can buy special Stanley Smartpants merchandise, you know T-shirts and Fridge Magnets, with illustrations of their favourite Cat-Haven Cat-Police characters on them. As I've said, Chief, even you!"

"It's amazing that a Sergeant in the Cat-Haven Cat-Police has got a website at all, if you ask me."

"Have a look at it, there's bound to be something to interest you!"

It was clear from the expression of amazement on Derek's face that he would never have thought of setting up his own website.

"Why don't you draw a chalk circle round the dead mackerel," said Stanley, "and then bag it up. I want to have a word with Peaches."

Whilst Derek was busy with the mackerel, Stanley spoke to Peaches. "I was wondering if you might like to help us with our cat-police work, Peaches. I have to follow up a clue at the Cluck Cluck Chicken Diner. I thought I'd go and have a meal there. If you're free this evening ….. perhaps you might like to join me?"

"I'd love to, Stanley. That would be really nice."

Lil returned with a printout in her hand, which she gave to Stanley. "Here's a photo of the necklace, too."

"Good. Try not to upset yourself too much, Lil. We'll get it back for you. I'll see you tomorrow. Stay cool. Come, Chief, we have work to do."

On the way back to the cat-police station Stanley was silent for a long while, and then he jumped up, almost strangling himself on the seatbelt. "Finding that blue hair at Cat-Diamonds "R" Us has given me an idea. Did you notice how clean Granny Garbo's house was?"

Derek Dimwit looked puzzled. "I hear what you

say, Stan, but I don't understand. What do you mean …. clean?"

"Almost for sure she's vacuumed her bedroom since she found the mackerel bones. I mean, she didn't leave it where it was for us to examine at the cat-crime scene, did she? She took it to the station."

"Was she going to catch a train, Stan?"

"Not a train station, Chief. *Our* station, the cat-police station." He fell silent once more and listened to the thrum-thrum of the windscreen wipers as the rain continued to lash down. "You know what I think, Chief?" he said after a while. "I think this mackerel business is a red herring."

"Now you're confusing me, Stan. What kind of fish is it? Is it a mackerel or a herring? And if it's a herring, how do you know what colour it is?"

"A red herring is something that the criminal-cat uses in order to send the cat-police in the wrong direction. In our case the criminal-cat has got us thinking about the death of a mackerel, instead of the real crime."

Chief Inspector Dimwit looked completely clueless. "I don't get it, Stan. What's the real crime?"

"Robbery, Chief. Robbery!"

Derek thought for a moment or two before speaking. "But there was no robbery at Granny Garbo's, was there?"

"My guess is that you're wrong about that, Chief. In fact, I'll bet you a couple of pints of cat-beer at the Cat and Fiddle that Granny Garbo *was* robbed. She just doesn't realise it. She's probably got an old shoebox under the bed, stuffed with cat-euros. That's what old grannies do, keep squintillions of cash at home so they can give it to their grandchildren when they visit. At least, the shoebox *was* stuffed with cash. I'll bet it's empty now! I think you should go back and see Granny tonight. Take Jumping Jack with you. I'm following up the mackerel trail at the Cluck Cluck Chicken Diner later."

"What do you want me to do at Granny's?"

"Firstly, we should take away her vacuum bag for examination. Secondly, we need to establish whether any money was stolen from her house. Was the mackerel a red herring?"

"This case is full of mackerel and herrings of one sort or another," said Derek Dimwit solemnly.

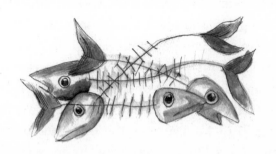

Friday 7th July

Later that summer's evening Stanley Smartpants called for Pretty Peaches in his own car, a shiny red E-Type Jaguar. She lived in Cat-Haven Towers, a large apartment block on the sea front. He took the elevator to the fifth floor, and examined his appearance in the mirror. From his collection of very smart and fashionable trousers, he had chosen to wear his special luminous green ones, with a matching bow tie and a green and black check waistcoat. His black shoes were perfectly polished.

He licked his paw and cleaned the back of his head, careful not to wash the sides of his face. He didn't want to rub off the expensive aftershave he was wearing, Brut for Cats. As the bell announced the elevator's arrival at the top floor, he took one final, admiring look at himself in the mirror. "Purrfect," he muttered.

Pretty Peaches was a peach marbled Australian Mist, with a lovely peach coloured face and deep gold, almond shaped eyes. She made martinis for them and they sat out on the terrace enjoying the magnificent view out over Cat-Haven Bay, watching the sun disappear beyond the hilltops.

The Cluck Cluck Chicken Diner was a fairly basic restaurant, decorated in blue and gold. A waiter-cat, a Blue Burmese, showed them to a table in the far corner of the room. His blue coat had a distinctive silver sheen and his eyes were a golden yellow. He had a heavy limp, dragging his left foot along the ground.

"Not a very exciting place, is it?" said Stanley. "Still, anywhere's nice when I'm with you."

Pretty Peaches smiled. The sound of Stanley's voice made her go weak at the knees. It was rich and deep, warm and friendly, and as smooth as the softest velvet. "You say the nicest things, Stan," she said.

Stanley looked around, his fully trained cat-police eyes taking in every detail. At the next table sat a father and his two kittens. They were on their starter course of green pea soup and crusty bread. Suddenly a strange gurgling noise came from the throat of the female kitten. Then her whole body jerked in a spasm of vomiting. A river of sick spewed out of her mouth straight into her bowl of green pea soup. Splodges of yellow-green liquid splashed onto the white tablecloth.

"Yuck!" exclaimed Peaches.

Stanley grimaced and wrinkled his nose distastefully. "I think we'll give the green pea soup a miss, Peaches, don't you?"

As soon as the waiter-cat returned with the menus, Stanley fished in his trouser pocket, took out his wallet and removed his warrant card. "I'm Detective Sergeant Smartpants of the Cat-Haven Cat-Police," he said. "Perhaps you would be kind enough to inform the manager-cat that I'd like to have a word with him."

Moments later a large black fat-cat approached their table. In fact he was so fat he was like a giant balloon ready to burst. It seemed to Stanley that he had eaten too many of his own chicken dinners. He was a Norwegian Forest Cat with a thick coat of shaggy black fur. Close up, the black colour was more of a dirty brown, and there was something odd looking about him too. It was only when he was standing at their table that Stanley realised that he had one terribly obvious glass eye. His good eye was a glowing gold.

"I'm Larry Cluck Cluck, the fat-cat owner of the business," he said self-importantly. "How can I help you, Sergeant?"

"I understand that a few days ago you bought some mackerel from Miss Ping Pong in the Fish Market."

"Yes."

"Have you had any go missing?"

"Funny you should ask that. It occurred to me only

yesterday that we had less mackerel than I thought. So I counted how many we had in the freezer."

"And?"

"There were six missing."

"Are you sure about that?"

"Yes."

"Were there any signs of a break-in?"

"Not that I could see."

"Could it have been one of your staff, Mr Cluck Cluck?"

"Difficult to say, but one odd thing did happen two days ago. My dishwasher-cat suddenly upped and left. He told me he'd got a better job, with more money."

"Do you suspect him of stealing the mackerel?"

"At the time I didn't know that any of the mackerel had been stolen. But I did wonder about him when I discovered the theft."

"What can you tell me about him?"

"Not much really. He's a Russian immigrant. I didn't like him. I thought he was disrespectful."

"What's his name?"

"I don't know his real name. I called him Beastly Boris."

"Can you give me his home address please, Mr Cluck Cluck."

"Well …… "said Larry Cluck Cluck hesitantly, "…. the thing is ….. I don't really know." His fat lips quivered alarmingly, and beads of sweat broke out on his forehead.

"What are you trying to tell me, Mr Cluck Cluck?" said Stanley. "Did you employ him illegally?"

Larry Cluck Cluck was silent, and his knees were trembling.

"We'll come back to this at a later date, Mr Cluck Cluck. Do you know anything about his new job?"

"Not exactly. But from a couple of things he said my guess is that he's gone to work at that Chez Les Chats place, that *French restaurant*." He stressed the words 'French' and 'restaurant' in a scornful voice.

At this, Pretty Peaches interrupted. "What's wrong with a French restaurant? A bit too up-market for the owner of a cheap chicken takeaway?"

Larry Cluck Cluck's fat face flushed a bright red and he reacted angrily. "There's nothing wrong with a chicken takeaway, you cat-fishwife!"

"Miaow, miaow," hissed Peaches through clenched teeth. "Your trouble is you've got no class, you blubbering puffed up fat-cat. You're stuffed up with too much cheap, greasy chicken!"

Secretly Stanley was thrilled by Peaches' blast at the pompous Mr Cluck Cluck. But he intervened smoothly. "Just a few final questions, Mr Cluck Cluck. Is Beastly Boris long-haired or short-haired? What sort of a cat is he? And what colour is he?"

"I think he's a Russian Shorthair, although I'm not sure. He's certainly got short hair, and his coat is a sort of blue colour."

Inwardly Stanley was elated at this piece of news. It seemed that he had a genuine suspect. But his outward demeanour did not change. "Did you ever see him wearing grey jeans?"

"Not that I recall."

Stanley was silent.

"Is that all?" Larry Cluck Cluck finally asked.

Stanley nodded. "For the moment."

"Would you like me to send over the waiter-cat to take your order?"

Pretty Peaches laughed out loud. It was a shrill, mocking laugh that almost cut Larry Cluck Cluck in half. "You must be joking! We've already seen what your food does to your cat-customers! And anyway, if you think we're going to eat here after you've insulted me you must be even more stupid than you look!" She got up from her chair and swished her tail scornfully. "Come on, Stanley, let's go and have a decent meal at Chez Les Chats. Let's leave this strutting fatty to his cheap, greasy chicken dinners. I bet he even waters down the wine." With that withering comment she strode away from the table. As they left the diner she turned to Stanley and spoke in a low voice. "Sorry about that outburst, Stanley. I hope it didn't upset your plans."

"It's OK, I'd finished with him. In fact, you just inspired me to make up a poem."

"Go on then," said Peaches eagerly.

****

"If for a meal to the Cluck Cluck Diner you go,
You'll find that their standards are decidedly low.
For they water the wine,
Which is not at all fine.
You're in for a shock and there's no whisker lickin',
It's just awful and vile and greasy old chicken!"

"That's great, Stanley!" Peaches clapped her paws together in delight. "It so upset me the way he said the words *French restaurant* in that dismissive tone of voice. My mother's French, and believe it or not she has a restaurant on the outskirts of Paris."

"What exactly does Chez Les Chats mean, Peaches? I don't know *much* French, although I do know that chat is French for cat. "

"It means The Cats' House, Stan. I'm looking forward to this. The food's great there."

Friday 7th July

They were shown to a candle-lit table, tucked away in a romantic corner of the Chez Les Chats restaurant. Their waitress-cat was a terribly pretty Turkish Angora with grey, blue, black, and white fur, large purple eyes and an enormous bushy tail that dragged along the ground as she walked. She was wearing a black silk cocktail dress and a garland of bright yellow feathers on the crown of her head. She was a student at Catford University, home for the summer holidays. She was studying Portuguese and tree surgery, an unusual combination it's true, but her long-term career plan was to be a lumberjack in Brazil.

"I just love those feathers," said Peaches. "Where did you get them?"

"Oh, that was a really wicked adventure! I caught a canary two weeks ago, and had lots of fun with it before

I killed it. I stripped off its feathers and gave them to my Mum. She's a genius with a sewing machine. And this was the result. It's cool, isn't it?" She took off the garland and passed it to Peaches.

"Can I try it on?"

"Of course you can."

Carefully Pretty Peaches put the garland on her head, and turned to Stanley. "How do I look?"

"You look lovely. That is soooo cool!"

Peaches gave the garland back to the waitress-cat. "What's your name?"

"They call me Gorgeous Gloria."

"Gosh, that really suits you."

"Thank you. My given name was Smokey. Can you believe that?"

"Humans are so unoriginal, aren't they?" said Stanley.

"I bet all the young tomcats are chasing you, you look so gorgeous," said Peaches.

"I do quite well." Gloria smiled, and gave them the menus. "Can I get you both an aperitif?"

"I'll have a martini," said Peaches.

"And I'll have a sherry," said Stanley. As Gloria walked away he suddenly laughed.

"What?"

"I was just thinking about my chief. He's such a dumb cat. For sure he doesn't know that an aperitif is a drink to sharpen the appetite before dinner. If he had been here, when the waitress-cat asked if we wanted an aperitif, do you know what he would have said?"

Peaches shook her head.

"He'd have said, why would I want a pair of teeth?"

Peaches howled with laughter, and Stanley did too. In fact, he laughed so much he had to clutch his ribs.

"You are funny, Stan!"

"Shall we start with garlic snails?"

"Yuck, no! I haven't had snails since I was being wined and dined in The Ritz Hotel in Paris by a French fashion designer-cat. You've probably heard of him, Jean-Paul Cattier. I used to be a model, you know, when I was younger, and I appeared on the catwalk in all the top fashion shows in Europe. Ah, yes," she sighed, "happy days! Anyway, this particular night we ordered snails. One of mine was still alive and he crawled across my plate, lifted up his head and looked straight at me. Then he spoke in a curiously squeaky voice. 'You wouldn't really eat a poor, defenceless snail, would you?' he squeaked. "As you can imagine I was shocked. I didn't know snails spoke cat-lingo. Well of course I didn't eat him, or any of his friends, and I've never eaten snails to this very day."

"Well OK, let's play safe and have a prawn cocktail."

Gorgeous Gloria returned with their drinks. "Have you decided?" she asked.

Peaches didn't answer the question. Instead she

asked a question of her own. "Who's performing tonight, Gloria?"

"Oh, it should be really good!" said Gloria excitedly. "It's the Red Hot Chilli Cats."

"Sorry to butt in," said Stanley, taking his wallet out of his trouser pocket. He flipped it open and extracted his warrant card. "Can I just ask you, Gloria, have you had anyone new working here in the last week?"

"Yes, we had a new dishwasher-cat who started just yesterday."

"What's his name?"

"He called himself Beastly Boris. But he didn't seem that beastly – he was terribly sweet to me."

"Anyone would be sweet to you, Gloria," said Peaches.

"Is he in the kitchen now?" asked Stanley.

"No, he didn't show up for work tonight."

"I see," said Stanley softly. "I'd better have a word with the manager-cat."

Stanley's wallet lay open on the table. Peaches couldn't help but see the photograph of a gorgeous Birman. She had a coat as white as dazzling snow, a dark brown face and electric blue eyes. Peaches looked enquiringly at Stanley.

"It was my mother," he said. "She was very beautiful, wasn't she?"

"Was?" said Peaches.

"Sadly she died a couple of years ago. She was my

best friend, Peaches. I miss her so much." Tears welled up in Stanley's eyes. "I loved her squintillions. Sorry, Peaches, I shouldn't have become so emotional."

"Don't be silly, Stanley. It's perfectly natural." A tear or two glistened in Peaches' eyes, and she dabbed at them with a hanky. "I haven't heard that word before, squintillions. I guess it means loads and loads?"

Stanley smiled. "Absolutely, Peaches. I made it up myself, especially for my mother."

"That's lovely, Stanley."

A large, fearsome-looking creature approached their table. He was a Havana Brown, his rich coat a deep mahogany brown, his eyes a bright green. He was impeccably dressed in a black dinner suit, and he was dripping with bling. He wasn't the most handsome of cats, for he had a broken nose and half of one ear missing. When he was younger he had been a professional boxer, and had fought for the World Cat-Heavyweight Championship. Early in the fight, the champion, Tuxedo Tyson, so called because he always fought in a black tuxedo, had bitten off a chunk of Frenchie's right ear. The fight was as good as over at that point. Frenchie was pawed, pounded, punched, pummelled, pulverized, and finally pole-axed by the brutal champion.

"Allo, good evening. Eet ees very nice to seeing you." he said in a strong French accent. "I am ze owner sir, Fearsome Frenchie. 'ow can I 'elp you?"

"I understand that you have recently employed a Russian Blue called Beastly Boris," said Stanley. "In the kitchen, perhaps?"

"Thees ees true. 'E started work 'ere yesterday, washing deeshes. But 'e 'as not arrived for work thees evening."

"I see. Do you have his address and telephone number?"

"I asked 'im for thees informations yesterday. 'E said 'e 'ad juss moved and 'e could not remember the address. 'E said 'e would tell me today, but 'e 'as not arrived for work."

"When should he have arrived?"

Fearsome Frenchie looked at his watch. "There is two hours."

Stanley frowned. "You mean two hours ago?"

"Of course. I 'ave 'ad experience of thees sorts of cats before. My guess ees 'e ees illegal immigrant. I do not expect to see 'im ever again!"

"Pliff," exclaimed Stanley with annoyance. "It seems we've missed him."

"Per'aps I can be 'elping you. When there ees a new person-cat, we always take 'is or 'er photograph, to put on our staff notice board. You can 'ave 'is photograph, Sergeant."

"Thanks. That's really helpful."

"I will ask Gloria to bring eet over to you. 'Ave you decided what you are going to order?"

"Yes, we have," said Peaches. "We're both going to

have a prawn cocktail to start, and then the pan fried sea bass with sauté potatoes. It sounds delightful."

"A very good choice," said Frenchie smoothly. "Our sea bass is ooh, la, la …." He kissed his paw and made a smacking sound with his lips.

Pretty Peaches smiled prettily. "And can we have a bottle of your finest French Chardonnay."

"Of course, but with the compliments of the 'ouse."

"That's soooo cool. Thank you, Frenchie," said Stanley.

Stanley had just put the last spoonful of ice cream in his mouth when his mobile phone bleeped and vibrated in his pocket. "Ah, it's a text from Jumping Jack." Peaches looked puzzled. "Sorry, Peaches. Of course you don't know Jack. He's one of my cat-constables. Oh, no, not another one!" He passed the phone to Peaches so that she could read the text.

Bad news 4 u. My sis just texted - robbery & dead mackerel at skating rink.

Saturday 8th July

"Shall we go to the skating rink, Chief?" said Stanley.

"Er ... well .... Stan," said Derek hesitantly, "I've got rather a lot to do, you know. Why don't you t-t-t-t-take Jack with you." He tried his best to stifle a yawn, but without success.

Stanley realised that what his boss really wanted was a sleep. "OK. Before we go, tell me what happened when you went back to see Granny Garbo."

"As you suggested I took Jack with me to help with examining the vacuum bag. We got lucky. The bag had almost nothing in it, so it made it easier to search. We did find a couple of blue hairs which we brought back to be examined."

"Good. We'll send them down to the lab. I wonder if they'll match the hair we found at Diamond Lil's?"

Just then there was a loud knock at Derek Dimwit's office door.

"Come in," said Derek.

Cat-Constable Jumping Jack bounded into the office.

"Good morning, Jack," said Derek.

Jack was practising a few jumps as he came into the room. Suddenly he leaped into the air and landed with a thump on Derek's desk. He turned towards Stanley. "See," he said proudly, "I told you I could do it!"

Chief Inspector Dimwit was unable to keep the smile off his face. He had a soft spot for little Jack, and allowed him to get away with almost anything. "Now look, Jack, you shouldn't jump onto my desk. You might disturb some important papers."

"Sorry, Chief." Jack grinned mischievously, not sorry in the slightest. He jumped around some more, doing a few somersaults, and generally having lots of fun.

"You're like a cat on a hot tin roof, Jack," said Stanley.

Jack jumped into the chair next to Stanley. "I was just practising. You never know when it might come in handy for catching criminal-cats. And anyway, my jumping skill paid off at Granny Garbo's."

"What happened, Jack?"

"Well, it was like this, Sarge. As we walked into Granny's bedroom, I was just practising a few jumps, pretending I was trying to catch a butterfly.

Suddenly I glimpsed something on top of Granny's wardrobe. It was an old shoe box. Granny said it had once contained a pair of beautiful shoes she'd bought in Hollywood." Jack scarcely paused to draw breath. He rushed on with his story, like a rubber ball bouncing out of control down a steep hill. "I jumped onto the dressing table, and from there onto the top of the wardrobe. The box was empty. And when I told Granny this she screamed. She cried out as if she'd caught her paw in a mousetrap. I've never understood why humans bother with mousetraps, when a cat can do the job so much better. Unless of course she's called Tammy! And what a terrible waste of good cheese." At last Jumping Jack paused to catch his breath. "Anyway, poor Granny was heartbroken. It turned out that the shoe box contained her life savings in cat-euro cash."

"Oh dear," said Derek. "Poor old Granny."

"Poor old grandchildren," said Stanley. "They won't get any dosh when they visit Granny. Jack, you're coming with me to the skating rink. We'd better get going."

The skating rink was close to the centre of the town, on the shoreline road, next to the Cat-Odeon cinema. Stanley and Jack walked through its circular swing doors.

The receptionist-cat was a Red Tabby LaPerm, and her coat was short and silky, and incredibly curly. She had just finished painting her claws, and she admired them now as she blew on them to help them to dry. She looked up as she heard approaching feet.

"Hello Jack," she said brightly. "Oooh, you're in uniform today. Is this an official visit?"

"Hello Scatty," replied Jack. "Haven't you heard about the dead mackerel you've found here?"

"No."

"Well, if you haven't heard about the dead mackerel, have you heard the one about the human judge who didn't have any thumbs?"

"No, I haven't."

"He was called Justice Fingers! Ha! Ha! Ha! So, who reported the dead mackerel?"

"Oooh, silly me! I was the one who rang the station! How could I have forgotten so soon?"

"We need to see the manager-cat, Scatty."

Scatty Patty picked up the office phone, and dialled a three figure number. There was no reply. "I'm sorry Jack, he's not answering. Oh, gosh and jolly hockey sticks! I forgot. It's his day off today. Silly me! Shall I ask Katie to come out?"

"Is she in charge today?"

Scatty Patty didn't answer, but dialled another internal number. "Katie," she gushed into the phone, "your brother Jack's here. Looking very handsome in his cat-police uniform, I must say!" There was a squeal of delight at the other end of the phone. Scatty Patty put the phone down. "I think she'll be out in a mo, Jack! Oh, look, here she comes now," she said, pointing with her mouth.

Skatie Katie had won the Figure Skating gold medal at the Winter Cat-Olympics in Bournemouth last year, and was now the resident skating coach-cat at the ice rink. She walked swiftly towards them. She was a stunning American Wirehair, and like Jumping Jack she had the same white blaze between the eyes and round the nose and mouth, but her tabby colouring was brown and grey. She had the same frizzy fur that stood up on end and bright shining hazel eyes. Stanley thought she was devastatingly attractive.

She rushed up to Jack and hugged him so hard, Stanley feared she might crush him. "Hello, I'm Sergeant Smartpants. Hope I'm not in the way!"

"Oh sorry," she said breathlessly, "it's just that I haven't seen Jack since ..... eight o'clock this morning! Of course I know you, I've seen your photograph in the Cat-Haven Cat-Police Gazette. Jack showed it to me only last week. I must say, you look even *more* handsome in the flesh! And it's obvious why they call you Smartpants. I just *love* those purple velvet trousers you're wearing. And that voice. Wow! I bet all the female police-cats fall in love with you just because of the sound of your voice." She switched on a dazzling smile.

Stanley blushed ever so slightly.

"I guess you've come about the dead mackerel," said Katie. "I expect you'd like to know where it was found. It was just down here, near the till. The person-cat who found it was Curious Connie."

"That's a curious name for a cat," said Stanley. "In fact it's silly. I mean, all cats are curious, aren't they?"

"There's no cat as curious as Connie," said Katie. "She was curious to find out what it would be like to be tumbled around in the washing machine, and washed all over. You know how long it takes most cats to clean themselves. Well, Connie thought that in the washing machine she could be cleaned all over in seconds. So she went to the cat-launderette, jumped into a machine and snuggled down amongst the clothes. Before long the manageress-cat set the controls for a long wash and turned the machine on. Connie was washed and cleaned, tilted and turned, jumbled and tumbled, rumpled and crumpled, and almost drowned. And just when she thought it had finished, the manageress-cat returned to start the drying cycle. Shock, horror! She saw Connie's frightened little face peering out from amongst the tangle of clothes. When Connie stepped out of the washing machine another shock was in store. The clothes she had curled up in were the football shirts of the Cat-Haven Gooners."

"And they play in red," said Stanley.

"Absolutely! So poor Connie ended up with pink and red patches all over her lovely white fur!"

Stanley laughed. "That's soooo cool! Nice story. It's not every day you see a red and white cat. Can we talk to her?"

"She's on her lunch break," volunteered Scatty Patty. "She's gone to CatDonalds for a double beef cat-burger and chips."

"I thought she was on a diet," said Katie. "Why is she eating junk food?"

"She had a good result this morning. When she weighed herself on the big weighing machine she found she'd lost three grams. She was just entering the figures on my computer here, when she saw the mackerel."

"Where is it now?" said Stanley

"It's right here," said Scatty.

"Where?"

"In front of me." Scatty Patty pointed at her computer with her mouth.

"Not your computer, Scatty. The mackerel!"

"Oh, silly me! It's in the bin over there." Once again she pointed with her mouth.

"I knew you'd want to see it where it was found," said Katie. "I told her she should have left it where it was."

Jack went over to the bin and picked up the fleshless mackerel carefully by the head. He swung it round in his mouth so that Stanley could get a good look at it. Apart from the head it had been picked clean. He put it down on the floor. "Shall I bag it up, Sarge?"

Stanley nodded. "Is there anything missing, Katie? Any money?"

Katie looked at Scatty Patty. "Have you checked the till, Scatty?"

"No."

While Katie and Scatty were checking the till Stanley and Jack searched for clues, and sure enough they found a single blue hair on the platform of the weighing machine.

"Do you think the criminal-cat weighed himself on the way out?" said Jack, tongue in cheek.

"Oh dear, Sergeant," Katie interrupted, "the till's almost empty. We've probably lost about two hundred cat-euros. Do you think there's a connection between the missing money and the mackerel?"

"It's a bit early to say, Katie. There is something you might be able to help us with however." He fished into the pocket of his purple and black striped waistcoat and took out the photograph of Beastly Boris. "Have either of you seen this cat?"

"Miaoooow! Miaoooow!" Both Katie and Scatty Patty squealed at the same moment.

"He was here this morning!" said Scatty.

"Yes, I skated with him," said Katie.

"Do you *know* him?" said Stanley, mild shock registering on his face.

"Of course I do. He's the Russian champion. I met him last year at the Winter Cat-Olympics in Bournemouth. He won the male-cats figure skating gold medal. We danced together at the Dinner and

Ball at the end of the Games."

"Beastly Boris was here this morning?"

Katie looked puzzled. "What do you mean? That cat's not Beastly Boris, he's Yuri Katakov."

It was Stanley's turn to look puzzled. "Are you sure this is the same cat? Please, Katie, look at the photo again."

Katie studied the photograph. "This is definitely Yuri Katakov. Look," she said, pointing with her paw. "He's got a piece missing from his right ear."

"How long did you skate with him?"

"About an hour. He was incredibly good. Did some amazing triple jumps. And a few quads!"

"Did you see him leave?"

"No. I had a lesson to give as soon as we finished skating. He said goodbye and left."

"Did *you* see him leave?" said Stanley, turning to Scatty Patty.

"No, I'm sorry."

"Shouldn't Curious Connie be back by now?"

It was Katie who replied. "Well, Sergeant, Connie likes to sleep a lot ......"

"Katie, please call me Stanley....."

Jack pounced. "Shall I call you Stanley too, Sarge?"

Stanley couldn't help but laugh. "Enough of your cheek, my lad!"

Katie continued, "..... and after she's been to Catdonalds .... Stanley, she usually goes off somewhere nice and warm and sleeps for a few hours."

"I see. Perhaps you could ask her to call me when she gets back. And if Yuri Katakov comes back, please ring me immediately."

"Of course I will, Stanley." Katie fluttered her eyelashes. "And if you want to ask me any more questions, I'm always available." She looked at Stanley meaningfully.

"There is one other thing. Could you put a list together of all your staff and any other cats who come here regularly. Thanks a lot, Katie. Stay cool."

Back at the station, Chief Inspector Derek Dimwit wandered into Stanley's office. I was just thinking about what you told me. I'm a bit confused, Stan. Are Yuri Katakov and Beastly Boris the same cat?"

"I think they must be."

"Well, do you think that this Yuri is using Beastly Boris as an alias to hide his true identity?"

"Interesting question, Chief. What I'd like to know is where he's been since the Cat-Olympics last year. Did he go back to Russia after the Games? And then come back here? Or has he been here all the time? Is he an illegal immigrant?"

"That's an awful lot of questions, Stan."

"Is he the thief-cat?"

"Well that's easy! Even a blind cat with a wooden leg could see that Beastly Yuri is the p-p-p-per... p-p-p-per ..... p-p-p-perper ...... the cat wot done the crimes!"

"Not necessarily. Although he is the prime suspect. What we can say is that we've got a serial thief on our paws."

"I hear what you say, Stan. But I don't get it. Why would he want to steal cornflakes?"

"Not that sort of cereal, Chief. I mean a cat who's robbed several victims."

"I knew that's what you meant. I'm not stupid. It was a joke, Stan. Anyway, it must be him. We know for a fact that he's been at the scene of two of the crimes, and we've found the same blue hairs at all three of the crimes. It *must* be him."

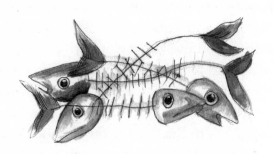

Saturday 8th July

There was a ring on the internal telephone. Stanley picked it up and listened to the voice at the other end. It was Greta the Grumbler, the cat-police station cook, who also fulfilled the role of Stanley's secretary.

"Is the chief free, Greta? …….. OK, it's probably best if you send her up to *his* office. Let him know what's happening, and tell him that Jack and I will be there right away." Stanley got up from his desk and stood in front of the full-length mirror to check how he looked. He admired his perfectly pressed purple velvet trousers, and smoothed down the fur on the top of his head. He buttoned the bottom button of his purple and black striped waistcoat, studied the effect for a few seconds, then unbuttoned it. He nodded his head briefly and smiled at his reflection.

He collected Jack from the Crime Room, and

together they went into Derek's office. "We've got a surprise visitor, chief," he said. "Gorgeous Gloria from the Chez Les Chats restaurant."

"Shut the door, Jack," said Derek Dimwit. "It's much more impressive if my door is shut when a visitor arrives. Gives Greta the chance to knock at the door and show a bit of respect."

A minute later Greta popped her head round the door. She hadn't bothered to knock. She was a Red Classic Tabby Maine Coon with white markings around the mouth and chin. She had a soft, glossy coat, a magnificent bushy tail and copper coloured eyes.

"I hate to complain, Chief, but surely one of the cadet-cats could have come down to collect Miss Gloria. I'm working my claws to the bone here. I have so much to do. Nobody has a clue how busy I am."

"Yes, thank you, Greta," said Derek.

Neither Jumping Jack nor Derek Dimwit had seen Gorgeous Gloria before, and they both gasped as Greta stood back to show her in. She looked absolutely gorgeous, her beautifully coloured fur and bushy tail taking their breath away. She was smartly dressed in a fashionably short blue denim skirt, which perfectly showed off her slim, graceful legs, and a white sweater. But the effect was stunning. She smiled as the three male cats almost fell over themselves, and each other, in their eagerness to show her to a chair.

Stanley made the introductions: "Gorgeous

Gloria, this is Chief Inspector Derek Dimwit .... and this is Cat-Constable Jumping Jack. What brings you here, Miss Gloria?"

"I thought I ought to come and tell you straightaway. Beastly Boris has been in touch."

"B-b-b-b.... Beastly Boris?" stammered Derek. "When? How? Why? Where?"

"That's an awful lot of questions," mumbled Jack.

"He rang me on my mobile phone," said Gloria. "About an hour ago. He invited me out to dinner tonight."

"G-g-g-g-g-g .... goodness g-g-g-g-g-g ... gracious!"

"Jumping Jellybeans!" said Jack.

"Did you accept?" asked Stanley.

"Of course, Sergeant. I knew you'd want me to. To be honest I don't find him very attractive, not like you guys!"

The three male cats purred contentedly. Derek blushed, while Stanley puffed out his chest. Jack assumed that she was referring only to him, and winked at her outrageously, a trick he'd learned from Stanley.

"We'll have to organise a stake-out," said Stanley.

"How do you know he's taking her out for a steak dinner?" queried Dimwit.

Stanley laughed. "I'm not talking rump steak and chips, Chief. Which reminds me, it'll soon be time for lunch! I mean we'll have to organise a surveillance team to watch over Miss Gloria."

"What's a surveillance team, Stan?"

"Chief, surveillance means close observation of a suspect."

"I realise that, Stan. Anybody would think I was stupid or something. I mean what sort of team?"

"I'll put together a small group of cat-detectives to keep an eye on Miss Gloria," said Stanley patiently. "What exactly have you arranged with Beastly Boris, Miss Gloria?"

"We're meeting at eight o'clock outside the National Catminster Bank in the High Street."

"Maybe now he's planning to rob the bank," ventured Derek.

"Right, Jack," said Stanley, "I want you to go and round up six cat-constables for this operation. Plus you and me, that makes eight. We'll need two cars from the motor pool."

"Don't you want me on this one, Stan?" said Derek, looking hurt.

"Of course you can be on it, Chief. Sorry, I didn't think of it. You don't usually come on this sort of operation."

"Well, this one's a bit different." Derek stole a glance at Gloria, and blushed.

"We'll sort it out later, Chief, after Miss Gloria has left. Jack, tell everyone we'll meet in the Crime Room at six o'clock. Off you go, now."

Jack looked dejected. "Oh, I thought you'd want me to take Miss Gloria home."

"I'll take care of that thank you, Jack. Off you go now, there's a good cat."

"OK, but before I go I've got a joke for you. A cat took his Alsatian dog into the pub with him. The dog was wearing snazzy blue socks and brown boots on all four paws. The cat went up to the bar to order a drink. 'I've never seen a dog wearing boots before,' said the barcat. It looks really odd. Why is he wearing brown boots?' 'Well usually he wears black ones,' said the cat, 'but they're at the menders!' Ha! Ha! Ha!"

As he went past Gloria, Jack leaned towards her and smelled her delightful perfume at close quarters. "Hope you liked the joke, Gloria." He gave her a huge wink. "And I hope we meet again."

Gloria gave Jack an encouraging smile.

Friday 7th July

Stanley Smartpants had decided that all the cats on duty should attend the six o'clock meeting in the Crime Room. He hoped that it would prove educational for the young cat-constables and cadet-cats who had not been selected for the Beastly Boris operation. They sat round a large wooden table, and each cat had a cup of tea and two chocolate biscuits in front of him.

Derek had insisted that he, and not Stanley, would make the opening address, and sit at the head of the table. In that way it would at least appear to the young cats that he was in charge of the operation. For reasons best known to himself he had changed into his camouflage combat shorts, thick knee length green socks which were stuffed untidily into large, black climbing boots, and a green-grey sweater.

"Now look here, cats," he began, "I want this

operation to go like clockwork. I've asked you all to wear dark casual clothes because I don't want Beastly Boris to be scared off at the sight of so many police-cats in uniform. Stanley and I will mastermind the operation from the CMCCR. And now he'll take you through the plan."

"What's the CMCCR?" queried one of the new cadet-cats.

"It's sooooo cool," said Stanley. "It's the Cat-Haven Mobile Computer Control Room. Or put more simply, it's a clapped out old van with a second-hand Amstrad computer that's always crashing!"

Several of the other cats laughed. Marmaduke used the distraction to whisper to Jack. "He's havin' a laugh isn't he, wearing those camouflage shorts? And with legs like that he's likely to scare anybody!"

All the male police-cats stood up and stared as Gorgeous Gloria was shown in by Greta, who was mumbling unhappily under her breath. Jack had just dunked a chocolate biscuit in his cup of tea, and was moving it rapidly towards his mouth. As he twisted his head round to look at Gloria, the biscuit thudded into his nose, wet chocolate side first. But he took no notice, dropped it on the table, and jumped up out of his chair. He almost ran towards Gloria. "Come and take a seat here, Miss Gloria," he said, pointing his paw towards the end of the table.

Gloria blushed. "Thank you, Jack." She looked

gorgeous in a pink skirt and white blouse.

Not one of the young male cats in the room took his eyes off her. Most of them started licking their fur. It was obvious that they all fancied her. The females looked on knowingly.

"Why are all you cats preening yourselves?" said Derek Dimwit.

"Come on, Chief, it's a normal thing to do," said Stanley.

> *"If you see a cat that's preening,*
> *Don't expect a deeper meaning.*
> *For sure it's just that he is keen*
> *To simply end up nice and clean!"*

All the police-cats round the table, males and females, smiled, and so did Gloria. "I'd like to use this opportunity," continued Stanley, "to thank Miss Gloria for agreeing to help us to catch Beastly Boris. It's very brave of you, Gloria. Right, the plan is very simple. We arrest Boris as soon as he shows his face. There'll be seven of you out on the street, and only one of him, so it should be easy."

"You can't fault Stan when it comes to numbers," said Derek for no apparent reason, other than to let everyone know that he was contributing.

"I just want to remind you all," continued Stanley, "to do nothing that might put Miss Gloria at risk of injury. Concentrate on the job at all times. Be alert and aware of everything that's going on. Two unmarked cars will take you all to the High Street. Miss Gloria will come with me and the Chief in the CMCCR, and we'll take up our position half an hour before Boris is due to arrive. In a few minutes cat-constable Jumping Jack will show you on the whiteboard where you will all be positioned. That's all, cats. Good luck!" Stanley jumped down from his chair. "Come to my office Miss Gloria, I want to explain to you exactly what we'd like you to do."

Jack looked on with disappointment as Stanley and Gorgeous Gloria left the room. Derek didn't really know whether to go with them or not. He followed them slowly to the door, and then sat down in the middle of the doorway, neither out nor in, unable to make a decision.

An hour and a half later the CMCCR was parked in the High Street a hundred metres from the NatCat bank. Inside it sat Stanley, Derek, Gloria, and a female cadet-cat. They had a perfect view of the bank on a large television screen.

"Time to go, Miss Gloria," said Stanley gently. As Gloria looked towards him, Stanley caught a sudden flash of fear in her large purple eyes. "Don't worry, we have all the latest up to date technology, and there are seven cats out there sworn to protect you. And remember, I'm here too, keeping an eye on you. And so is Chief Inspector Dimwit."

Gloria left the van and walked purposefully towards the bank, her bushy tail swishing behind her. Stanley cast his eyes round the High Street, trying to pick out his police-cats. Shock, horror! He saw two of his cats in the side street coming out of Catdonalds, stuffing their faces with double beef cat-burgers and chips. And when he looked over to the other side of the road, he saw another two of his cats, fast asleep on the comfy-looking bed in the furniture shop window. "Pliff!" he exclaimed. "What are they all doing?"

And then, to make matters worse, a Securicat van pulled up outside the bank. It completely blocked his view, and he lost sight of Gloria. A taxi arrived, a door opened, and a cat's paw could be seen beckoning furiously. The paw was blue!

When Gloria saw Boris beckoning to her from the taxi, she looked back towards the van. She didn't know what to do. Her view of the van, and the van's view of her, was blocked. She looked around desperately, hoping to see one of the police-cats, but there was no-one. She began to sweat. She felt sick. Panic gripped her. And Boris was still beckoning, trying to get her to cross the pavement and jump into the taxi.

Stanley knew that he had to act fast. He leaped out of the van, and ran towards the bank. He clearly saw Beastly Boris, who had by now got out of the taxi and was walking towards Gloria. Unfortunately Derek Dimwit also leaped from the van and ran a few paces behind Stanley. Boris turned round. It was the sight of two cats running towards him, one of them wearing camouflage combat shorts and serious black boots, that told him that something was wrong. He raced back towards the taxi. But Stanley was almost on him. Boris swung round and cuffed Stanley on the side of the head, catching him off balance and knocking him backwards. He managed to stay on his feet just long enough to take the impact of Derek Dimwit crashing into him. Both cat-police fell to the ground. As Stanley jumped up Boris threw himself into the taxi, and slammed the door shut. With a screech of tyre rubber the taxi sped off towards the sea.

Stanley was breathing hard, and his nose was bleeding. Gloria ran towards him and threw her front paws round his neck. "Are you all right, Stanley?" she cried, and licked the side of his face.

"I'm fine, Gloria. I'm so sorry for this fiasco."

Derek Dimwit got to his feet. "Sorry, Stan, it was my fault he got away. I should have stayed in the van as you asked me to."

At that moment Jack and four of the cat-constables came strolling round the corner, each one of them licking his lips and preening himself.

"You've all been to Catdonalds!" said Stanley incredulously. "Why are you eating when you're on duty?"

"We get hungry on duty," replied Jack. "It seemed like a sensible idea to eat something before the operation, in case we wouldn't get the chance later."

"Well you won't get the chance at all now. The operation's already over. Boris has been and gone!"

"Oh dear," said Jack sheepishly.

"Thanks to the bungling stupidity of everyone involved in this operation, we've lost him. And worse than that, we've let him know that we're after him. We may never get as good a chance again!"

Monday 10th July

"This should put the cat amongst the pigeons, Stan," said Chief Inspector Derek Dimwit, throwing a copy of the Cat-Haven Chronicle onto Stanley's desk.

The Cat-Haven Chronicle
Published by Sky-Cat Enterprises
Monday 10ᵗʰ July 2006   *1 Cat-Euro*

MACKEREL ROBBERIES MYSTERY
An outbreak of dead mackerel in Cat-Haven-on-Sea has mystified the cat-police. According to a reliable cat-police source, an undisclosed number of mackerel skeletons has been discovered at the scene of several robberies. The Cat-Diamonds "R" Us jewellery store in the High Street and the

Cat-Haven Skating Rink are known to have been robbed. It is also believed that dear old Granny Garbo, former Hollywood superstar-cat, has also been robbed by the heartless, worthless villain.

Suspicion has fallen on a Russian Blue, and current Cat-Olympic Ice Skating champion, Yuri Katakov. This cat is also know as Beastly Boris, and seems to be a part-time dishwasher. On the next page we publish his photograph, kindly supplied to us by the Chez Les Chats up-market French Seafood Restaurant. We understand that the cat-police wish to interview Beastly Boris in connection with these crimes, and came within a cat's whisker of capturing him on Saturday evening in a skilfully planned cat-police operation.

Continued on Page 2

"How on earth did they get this information, Stan?"

Stanley grinned. "They don't call me Smartpants for nothing, you know."

Derek looked at Stanley with envy in his heart. As usual Stanley was stylishly dressed. He was wearing pale grey cords, spangled with flecks of the colours of the rainbow. They were complemented by a silvery blue waistcoat and a multi-coloured bow tie in a kaleidoscope of circles and triangles, and on his feet he wore pale blue crocks.

"*I* gave them the information last night, Chief."

"I would *never* have thought of that."

"Let's just hope that the cat-public can find him for us."

There was a loud rap at the door, and Jumping Jack came leaping into the room, practising his jumps. He skidded to a halt in front of Stanley's desk. "There's been another robbery, Sarge," he said.

"Where?" said Stanley.

"At the Cat-Odeon cinema complex."

"Was there a dead mackerel?"

"They didn't say."

Stanley swivelled round in his desk chair and got to his feet. "Let's find out a bit more."

As Stanley, Derek and Jack walked into the Crime Room there was a loud shriek. A Black Smoke and White Cornish Rex leaped to her feet and clapped her paws together. She ran over to the coffee machine, her long, graceful legs flowing across the floor. She began to dance around it, swishing her hips from side to side and waggling her large, prominent ears. Cat-Constable Playful Pamela was proud of her curvaceous body and seized upon any opportunity to show off. She had a striking face with shades of blue and black and grey around a white mouth and chin, and a delightfully pink nose.

"I've got it!" she cried, her pretty face a picture of delight. "I know who the criminal-cat is!" She danced round and round. Tammy flicked on her iPod Shuffle, which was clipped to the waistband of her jeans. It was the SugaKittens latest hit, Easy Peasy. She and two of the female cadet-cats also began to dance, and sing along with the music.

"Come on baby, it's easy peasy!
Come on honey, it's easy peasy!"

Chief Inspector Dimwit smiled happily, thinking that his young cats were working hard on one of the unsolved cases.

"I've got it!" said Pamela again. "I accuse Colonel Mustard in the dining room with the dagger!"

Derek's expression changed in an instant, and his face turned purple. He began to tremble. "What on earth are you cats doing?" he shouted. "You're supposed to be working on the case of the p-p-p-p-p-p.... plumber and the stolen radiators, not playing stupid b-b-b-b-b-b....board games."

Playful Pamela blushed. "I'm sorry, chief, we *are* working on it, it's just that ..."

"I hear what you say, Pamela, but that's enough. I don't want any excuses. This is c-c-c-c-c-completely unacceptable behaviour. You four cats will have extra training this morning, and you'll have to m-m-m-m-m-m-miss today's lunch."

"Oh, that's so unfair," cried Tammy Tickletummy. "I'm always hungry. All the time. I need my lunch. I'm a growing cat. You can't do this. It's not fair!" Her lips quivered uncontrollably, and tears glistened in her startlingly blue eyes. "And we've got rhubarb pie and custard. It's my favourite! It's not fair. It's in breach of my cat rights in the workplace." Suddenly she threw herself on the floor and lay down on her back, all four paws in the air.

Pamela, who was a kind and caring cat, and Tammy's best friend, came over and knelt down beside her. "Don't upset yourself, Tammy. The nasty Chief Inspector doesn't mean it. Of course you'll get your rhubarb pie. Here, let me tickle your tummy."

Derek turned a deeper shade of purple, and it seemed to Stanley that he was on the verge of exploding.

"The Chief's right," he said. "This just isn't good enough. There's a time and place for everything.

Playing a game when you should be at work,
It just makes you look a bit of a jerk.
For fooling around there is not the time.
We're trying to solve the mackerel crime.

Now stop this nonsense. The Chief is perfectly within his rights to ask you to do extra training. But if you work hard for the rest of the morning,

I'm sure he'll let you all have your lunch. Let's all get back to work."

One of the cadet-cats jumped up from his chair. It was Vacant Vincent, so called because he seemed to spend most of his time staring into space, a vacant expression on his face. Vincent was a Black and White Manx. He was a rumpy, that is to say a Manx who had no tail. But his lack of a tail was not his only problem.

"I'm sorry about this, Sarge," he said with a pained expression on his face, "but I need to go for a poo!"

"Well, don't be long, Vincent," said Stanley.

Vincent ran towards the door, his bunny-hop gait causing much amusement amongst the other cats.

"Not again," said Jack. "He's always going to the toilet. I know what. Why don't we call him Vinnie the Poo? Ha! Ha! Ha!"

Several cats laughed out loud. "Good one, Jackster," said Marmaduke.

"You shouldn't laugh at Vincent for something he can't help," said cadet-cat Studious Stephen. "Both his parents were rumpies you know, and as a result he suffers from Manx Syndrome. Not many cats know this, but Manx Syndrome is a potentially fatal bowel disorder."

This last remark was greeted in near total silence. Stephen toyed with his wire-framed nose glasses, proud to show off his knowledge in front of the other cats. He was a Blue Cream and White Devon

Rex, quite tall with long, slender legs that seemed slightly bowed. He had a scrawny neck and a round, chubby face. Most of the female cats thought that he was very unattractive.

"Who took the telephone call from the Cat-Odeon?" said Stanley.

"I did," said Marmaduke. "I was just eating my toast and marmalade when the phone call came in ....."

"Spare us the breakfast details, Marmaduke, for heaven's sake," said Stanley. "Who did you speak to there?"

"The manager-cat"

"And what exactly did he say?"

Marmaduke consulted his notebook, and made a great play of flipping over the pages. "Let me see," he said slowly and deliberately. "Ah yes, here it is ..... and I can quote his words exactly."

Stanley sighed a deep sigh. "Get on with it, Marmaduke," he muttered.

"Yes, his exact words were .... we've had a robbery ..."

"Is that all?"

"No, Sarge, then he said .... we've lost our entire weekend takings. And then *I* said .... I see ..... and then *he* said .... it's a lot of money .... and then *I* said .... when did this happen? .... and then *he* said .... if I knew the answer to that question, I would have caught the thief .... and then *I* said ...

"For heaven's sake, Marmaduke," interrupted Stanley, "stop saying *I* said *he* said. Just give me the facts!"

"Right, Sarge. Just a moment." Marmaduke delved into his trouser pocket and took out a marmalade-coloured handkerchief. He blew his nose noisily, waking one of the cadet-cats who had fallen asleep. "The theft was discovered early this morning. The safe was broken into, and they think they've lost about 2000 cat-euros. And one other thing ..." He paused to make sure that he had every cat's attention. "There was a skeleton of a dead mackerel lying inside the safe."

"Jack, I'd like you and Marmaduke to go to the Cluck Cluck Diner and investigate their employee records. Check out that all the staff working there today are legal, and take a note of any that aren't. And keep your eyes open for any suspicious characters. The Chief and I are going to the Cat-Odeon."

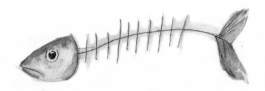

Monday 10th July

S tanley parked the panda car in one of the designated parking spaces outside the Cat-Odeon. The first thing they saw was a huge poster advertising one of the current films.

SCREEN ONE
The Cat-Odeon, Cat-Haven-on-Sea
Sponsored by Cat-Tucky Fried Chicken
"It's whisker licking good!"
proudly presents
CAT TITANIC
Starring
Lionardo di Catrio & Kat Winslett
and a supporting cast of multi-talented cats
Directed by Stephen Spielcat

They entered the building to find themselves in a huge carpeted foyer. There was a soft drinks bar to their left. "Shall we have a Cat-Cola, Stan?" said Derek Dimwit.

"Maybe later, Chief." Stanley went over to the glass-fronted box office. "We've come to see the manager-cat," he said to the female cat who seemed to be in charge. "I'm Detective Sergeant Smartpants of the Cat-Haven Cat-Police. The manager's expecting us. Here's my ID." He produced his warrant card, and the receptionist-cat picked up the telephone.

They were shown into the manager-cat's office, which was on the top floor of the building, and one floor above the nine cinema screens. Miserable Melvin got up from his swivel chair and crossed the room to shake paws with his visitors. He was a shorthaired Abyssinian, with a seriously turned down mouth and large protruding eyes. He certainly *looked* miserable. "Good morning, gentlecats," he said, his voice dripping with misery. "This is an even more miserable start to a Monday morning than usual."

"Quite so. I'm Detective Sergeant Smartpants, and this is my colleague Detective Chief Inspector Dimwit. Let's get straight down to business. Where was the money stolen from?"

"Right here, from my wall safe. I've left it exactly as I found it when I came in this morning. As you can see the door of the safe is hanging off its hinges. The one thing I don't understand is why the thief-cat left the skeleton of a dead mackerel in it."

"There don't seem to be any signs of forced entry, Melvin. Was your office door left open?"

"No, I locked it last night, and it was still locked when I came in this morning. But the window was open. Perhaps I forgot to shut it last night before I left."

Derek walked over to the open window and looked out onto the street two storeys below. He examined the window frame. "Goodness gracious! It looks as though it's been forced, Stan. Look!"

Stanley went to have a look, and nodded his head in agreement. "It does *look* that way."

"The thief couldn't possibly have got in without climbing the wall or lowering himself from the roof. I guess this means he was a cat burglar, Stan!"

Stanley ignored Derek's joke. "Does any other cat have a key to your office, Melvin?"

Melvin looked more miserable than a humanised cat whose bowl of cream has been taken away from him. "There's a spare key hanging on a nail in the projection room. All the cats on the staff know it's there."

Stanley shook his head in disbelief. "I think we'll have to undertake an advertising campaign, chief, to make our citizen-cats more aware of the importance of security." He turned back to Melvin. "What about the cleaners? Do they know about the key?"

"Of course they do. They need the key to get into my office to clean it."

"I know I'm not very bright," said Chief Inspector Dimwit, "but what's the point of locking your office door if every cat who works here has access to the key that opens it?"

"Very good question, chief," said Stanley.

Melvin looked even more miserable than a few moments ago.

"We'll need a complete list of all your staff, including casual staff, with all their personal details, and photographs where you have them."

"But that will take ages to put together."

"Do you want your cat-euros back or not? Why don't you start on the list, Melvin, while Chief Inspector Dimwit and I examine your office for clues."

Disappointingly, there were no hairs to be found in or around the safe. There *was* a pawprint on the door of the safe, however, which Stanley circled with a piece of white chalk. He was in little doubt that it would be an exact match for the one lifted from Granny Garbo's bedroom.

Miserable Melvin returned to his office and sighed a deep sigh, as if the world was about to end.

"Melvin," said Stanley, "I want you to make sure that no cats touch the evidence we've circled before our forensic cats come to examine it. How are you getting on with that list?"

"Give me a chance. It all takes time, you know. I've got the cleaners' file sorted out – it's in the downstairs office. I've only been able to find *some* of the Cat Resources file, which contains all the staff information. I'm not sure what's happened to the rest of it. I was wondering if perhaps there's a file in one of the drawers of my desk."

"Well, while you're completing the exercise, we're going over to the skating rink. We'll be back shortly to collect what you've managed to put together."

"You must be Curious Connie," said Stanley to the cat sitting behind the reception desk. "I heard about your encounter with the red football shirts!"

Connie was a pure White Longhair Scottish Fold. At least she *had been* pure white before the incident in the launderette. Now she was a curious mixture of red and white stripes and blotches. Even her folded over ears were red and white. The only part of her that was not red and white were her eyes, which were large, enquiring and olive green.

Stanley contrived an outrageous wink. Most cats were completely unable to wink, but Stanley had practised it for years. He'd taught Jack how to do it, and Jack was getting quite good at it. But he wasn't in Stanley's league. To see Stanley's hugely exaggerated wink was almost as big a treat as a chicken dinner at Cat-Tucky Fried Chicken. Stanley's charm didn't work on this occasion, for Connie was decidedly frosty. "Who wants to know?" she said.

"Sergeant Smartpants of the Cat-Haven cat-police. We've come to see Skatie Katie, and of course you. We missed you when we were here yesterday."

"Oh, sorry," said Connie. "I didn't realise." She picked up the telephone and dialled. "Katie," she said, "there's a Sergeant Smartsomething to see you."

There was a sharp intake of breath from the other end of the phone that was clearly audible. Stanley licked his paw and smoothed the fur on top of his head.

Moments later Katie appeared, looking slightly flustered. "Hello, Stanley," she said, purring contentedly. She gazed at him unblinkingly, her large hazel eyes like huge marbles. "What can I do for you?" She didn't take her eyes from his face for a second. Derek Dimwit looked on enviously.

"We're just passing by, but thought it would be nice to drop in and see you. Did you have a chance to get the list of staff for us?"

"Yes, it's all done and dusted. I thought that's why you had come. I left a message with Cheerful Charlie less than an hour ago. Before you go I'll pop up to my office and get it for you. "

"Good. I don't suppose you've got anything else for us?"

"Unfortunately not, but Connie might have

something of interest for you."

"It's probably nothing, Sergeant," said Connie, "but two days before the robbery, I noticed a cat hanging around, not really doing anything, just ..... you know ..... hanging around."

"Can you describe him?"

"I didn't really pay a lot of attention, I was on my way out to my lunch break."

"Anything would help, Connie."

"He was blue-grey, I'm sure of that, well almost sure. Maybe silvery blue"

"Any idea what breed he was?"

"No, I'm sorry."

"Anything else?"

"Sorry, Sergeant, I know I'm not being much help."

"Any particular characteristics that you noticed?"

"Come to think of he limped a bit, you know dragged one paw along the ground. At least I think he did."

Monday 10th July

After collecting Miserable Melvin's employee records, Stanley and Derek went to Cat Diamonds "R" Us. When they walked into Diamond Lil's office they found her stretched out on top of a high storage cupboard. She was crying, sobbing her heart out. Her eyes were puffy and her nose was running. There was almost a full box of used tissues beside her.

"Come on down from that cupboard, Lil, and tell me what's the matter," said Stanley gently.

Lil did as she was told and jumped down onto the floor. But she couldn't stop herself from crying.

Stanley moved towards her. "Come here, Lil." He put his paws around her and hugged her tightly. Neither of them spoke for a few moments.

It was Lil who broke the silence. "Oh, Stan, I'm ruined! My business insurance ran out the day before the robbery. I was so busy I forgot to renew it. I won't get a cat-euro for the necklace. I don't suppose you've found it?"

"No, Lil. I'm sorry. We haven't. But we will, I promise you."

"You can't promise that, Stan. I know you never find most things that have been stolen. I just know I'll never see it again."

"Let's be positive, Lil. Something will turn up."

Suddenly Lil brightened. "I've been so upset about the insurance that I'd almost forgotten what one of my staff told me this morning. Precious Gemma saw a cat wandering up and down outside the shop the day before the robbery."

"Would you like to ask her to come in, so I can talk to her about it?"

Lil picked up the phone on her desk. "Gemma, can you come into my office. Sergeant Smartpants of the Cat-Haven Cat-Police would like to have a word with you."

"You mustn't upset yourself so much, Lil. Don't give up hope. We've got a good team working on the case. Something will turn up. In the meantime, I'd like a copy of your staff records that we can take away with us."

"I don't think you'll get much from them. All my staff are known to me personally. I can vouch for all of them."

"I'm sure none of them is involved in this, Lil. But

we have to follow up everything, most often just to eliminate as many cats as we can. It's a bit of a drag, but it has to be done."

"I understand, Stanley, and I'm grateful that you're doing everything you can."

Precious Gemma came breezing into the room. She was an odd eyed White Turkish Angora, with pink ears and a pink nose. She was wearing the Cat Diamonds "R" Us uniform of pink skirt and silver-grey blouse. Stanley found himself staring at her eyes, for one of them was gold, and the other was blue.

"You love my eyes, don't you?" she said to Stanley directly.

"They're soooo cool!" Stanley smiled at her. "Let me introduce my boss, Chief Inspector Dimwit."

Derek leaned forward eagerly, but Gemma simply nodded indifferently, and spoke to Stanley. "What would you like to know, Sergeant?"

"Tell me about this cat you saw."

"A couple of days before the robbery, I saw a strange cat pacing up and down in the street, as if he was desperate for food. And he kept looking through the window. He seemed to be terribly interested in what was going on in the shop."

"Perhaps he was casing the joint," ventured Derek.

"Go on, Gemma," said Stanley.

"That was all really."

"How long was he there?"

"Oh, at least twenty minutes."

"Can you give us a description?"

"Of course."

"Good. Can you write this down please, Derek?"

Derek took out a notebook from his waistcoat pocket, and then a pencil. He licked it twice, as if to make sure it would write properly.

"He was a medium-sized shorthaired cat with brilliant green eyes," said Gemma positively.

"He was definitely a male cat, was he?" said Stanley.

"Yes."

"Do you know what breed he was?"

"No, but his coat was blue with a silver sheen."

"How was he dressed?"

"Pretty shabbily. He was wearing black trousers which were badly creased, and a white shirt that looked more grey than white."

"Would you recognise him if you saw him again?"

"I think so."

"Is there anything else?"

Precious Gemma frowned. "Not that I can recall. No, wait a minute. He had a rather heavy limp."

"I've had an idea, Derek," said Stanley when they were back in the panda car. "You remember that cat we went to see a few months ago. We called him Klepto Klaws. Squintillions of paintings had been stolen from Cat-Haven House, and we suspected *him* of handling them, but we couldn't prove anything."

"Yes, I vaguely remember."

"I think we'll go and pay him a visit, Chief. I've got a hunch."

"Did you say after lunch, Stan?"

"A hunch, Chief, a hunch! Mind you, lunch sounds like a good idea. Let's call in at the Cat and Fiddle on the way. I fancy steak and kidney pie and chips. With lots of gravy!"

Ten minutes later they walked into the Cat and Fiddle. It was well known for providing good meals at reasonable prices, and was therefore one of the most popular pubs in Cat-Haven-on-Sea. It was packed with business-cats having lunch.

"Isn't the air nice and clean in here," said Stanley. "now that they've banned cats from smoking in pubs, bars and restaurants. It's so much more healthy."

"I couldn't agree more, Stan. Smoking is such a filthy habit."

They were fortunate to find two high stools at the bar and ordered soft drinks. The food menu was on a huge chalkboard the length of one wall, and offered a variety of tasty meals and snacks. Suddenly there was a shriek of laughter from the far side of the bar. Two cats were playing pool, and one of them had just scooped a ball off the table with his cue. The ball bounced noisily on the stone floor. Stanley ordered his steak and kidney pie, and Derek chose a spaghetti Bolognese.

"A cat with a heavy limp could be the breakthrough we've been waiting for," said Stanley, swigging back his orange juice. "That's the second sighting of a blue cat with a limp. And by the sound of it he was checking out the premises a few days before the robberies. Surely it can't be a coincidence?"

"It does give us another suspect, Stan. As far as we're aware Beastly Boris doesn't have a limp."

"We'll check that with Katie later."

Derek would have preferred to have a sleep after lunch, but Stanley was anxious to catch up with Klepto Klaws. He lived in a large detached house near the top of Cat-Haven Hill. It was a corner property with a rockery-style front garden and a large back garden that went round three sides of the house. A huge kidney-shaped pond, in which Klepto kept lots of goldfish, was the main feature. In the vegetable section Klepto grew runner beans, cauliflower, broccoli, and peas. He also grew raspberries and blackberries. In the greenhouse he had tomato plants, and there was a cute little summer house where he could rest and soak up the sun. This was where they found him, stretched out in a hammock, having a sleep.

"Hello, Klepto. Remember me? Sergeant Smartpants of the Cat-Haven Cat-Police."

Klepto Klaws tilted his head, one of his bleary

eyes opening a fraction. The other was covered with a black patch. The story was that he had lost an eye during a fight with an Irish cat about whether or not a glass of Guinness a day was good for you. Klepto was a sphinx, a breed of cat not known for its beauty. In fact he was an ugly cat, black in colour, his body quite wrinkly and almost hairless, and his ears comically large.

"How did you get in?" he said aggressively. He yawned, opening his mouth so wide that you could see every tooth in his head.

"Well, we could have jumped over the gate," replied Stanley. "But we didn't need to. It was open. Any good paintings been through your hands lately?"

It was a loaded question, and Klepto knew better than to answer.

"We're here about the expensive diamond necklace that was stolen from Cat-Diamonds "R" Us."

"Yes, I read about it in the Cat-Haven Chronicle. I don't know what you think it's got to do with me. Anyway, I thought some Russian cat was the thief."

"I'm not suggesting *you* stole it, Klepto. But what I *am* suggesting is that you bought it from whoever did steal it."

"Rubbish!" spluttered Klepto. He had a guilty look on his face that did not escape the eagle eye of Stanley Smartpants.

"It's what you do isn't it, Klepto? Handle stolen property? We might get a search warrant."

"Suit yourself. You won't find anything here."

"There's another matter I want to discuss with you. What do you know about squintillions of radiators that went missing last week from that big house right at the top of the hill?"

"Maybe someone was cold and needed extra heating!"

"If I get my teeth into you, Klepto, believe me, clever remarks are not going to get you off the hook."

Klepto became more aggressive. "Are you accusing me of something? Because if you are, then I suggest you arrest me. And if you're not going to arrest me then get off my property. Go on, clear off!" He started to rise from his hammock.

Stanley realised that he wasn't going to get anything more from the conversation, and motioned with his paw. "You stay in your hammock, Klepto. I've finished with you for today. We'll see ourselves out. Oh, and by the way, you ought to improve your security, or you'll end up being the victim of a robbery."

"He's hiding something, Derek," said Stanley climbing into the car. "Did you notice the guilty look on his face when we were discussing the robbery at Cat-Diamonds "R" Us?"

"Matter of fact I did," replied Derek.

"And he was too quick to say we wouldn't find anything in his house, wasn't he?"

"I guess so. I wonder what he knows?"

"I *can* tell you one thing, Chief. He knows that a diamond necklace was stolen from Lil's."

"Of course he does, Stan. Everyone knows. Even a blind cat with a wooden leg would know that. As he said, it was in the Cat-Haven Chronicle."

"That's where you're wrong, Chief. It didn't mention a diamond necklace in the newspaper article. I particularly asked the editor-cat *not* to mention it."

"So how did he know?"

"That's a good question. And the answer is that he couldn't possibly know unless he's been told about the necklace, or he's seen it."

"That was very clever of you, Stan. We've got a hot lead at last. What are you going to do now?"

"I think perhaps we'll get Jumping Jack to follow Klepto tomorrow. See where he goes. See if he leads us to where he stashes his gear."

Tuesday 11th July

There was a light knock on Derek Dimwit's door. A tall mediterranean-looking cat, wearing a loose fitting white coat, entered the office. It was Francesca Forensicca, a beautiful brown Tonkinese. Her face and ears were a dark brown, and her coat was short and silky with varying shades of light brown. She had a long, dark brown tail and lustrous aqua-green eyes. She was an American cat of Italian descent who lived in Catmel-by-the-Sea in California, and was employed by the Catmel County Cat-Police Department.

She had agreed to be temporarily transferred to Britain. Sheriff Chuck Smartpants had said to her, "my cousin needs your help. He's a Sergeant in the Cat-Police in a real nice town in Britain, but they have no forensic expertise. I want you to set up a fully functioning forensic department. It'll take you several months, but I'm sure you'll enjoy it. And you'll get on with my cousin, Stanley. He's a real nice guy."

"Hey, chief, how you doin'?" said Francesca. "Hi Stan."

"Morning, Fran," said Stanley pleasantly.

"I'm doing just fine, Francesca," said Derek. "What have you got for us?"

Francesca put on a huge pair of spectacles that covered her entire face, and opened her folder. "The hair found at Cat-Diamonds "R" Us, and the two hairs from Granny Garbo's, are from the same cat. They're a perfect match. I haven't had time yet to examine the one from the skating rink, but I should know that tomorrow."

"Excellent," said Stanley, nodding his head with satisfaction. "Do you know what breed it is?"

"No, I haven't worked on that yet."

"I bet you it's a Russian Blue," said Derek.

"And what about the torn piece of grey cloth?" said Stanley.

"The only thing I can say for sure is that it's from a pair of jeans that were probably not made in Cat-Haven."

"I knew it!" said Derek. "I bet they were made in Russia."

"That's jumping the gun, Chief. But I should

102

know in a couple of days."

"What can you tell us about the three mackerel?" asked Stanley.

"They're dead, Stan!" Francesca chuckled. "Not a lot really, except that there's no flesh on any of them. We know that they were pan fried in garlic butter, shallots and white wine before they were eaten, though."

"Perhaps the thief was a trained chef," suggested Derek. "We can check out all the chefs and staff who had access to the kitchens in the Cluck Cluck Diner and Chez Les Chats."

"Good idea, Chief."

Chief Inspector Dimwit blushed ever so slightly. He was thrilled whenever Stanley gave him any praise or encouragement. "Stanley and I have just come back from the Cat-Odeon, Fran."

"Yes, I heard there'd been a robbery there, and another mackerel skeleton. Any clues?"

It was Stanley who answered Francesca's question. "We found a pawprint at the scene. Let's hope our forensic cats can lift a good image."

"Well, I'd better be off, Chief. I've got plenty to be working on."

"Thanks a lot, Francesca." It was common knowledge amongst his cat-police colleagues that Derek fancied Francesca, and he tried his best to give her a winning smile. He'd been practising it in the mirror in his bedroom for weeks.

Francesca nodded in return. "You're welcome, Chief."

As Francesca left the office Jumping Jack came bounding in. As usual he was jumping in the air trying to catch imaginary butterflies. He thought about leaping onto Derek's desk, but saw the disapproving look on the Chief's face and changed his mind. And then he spotted an empty cardboard box on the far side of the office. It was the box which had contained Derek's new LCD flat screen television, now sitting on top of the bookcase. Derek's reason for getting it was so that he could watch football and horse racing without having to go home or to the pub. Jack threw down the folder he was carrying and raced across the floor towards the box. With a flying leap he threw himself into it. First of all he sniffed every inch of cardboard, and then he started to run around inside the box, having loads of fun.

"For heaven's sake come out of there, Jack. We've got work to do!" said Derek.

Reluctantly Jack did as he was told, and jumped out of the box. But he couldn't resist making a comment. "You know what they say, Chief," he said, "all work and no play makes Jack a dull boy. Ha! Ha! Ha!"

"Yes Jack, I hear what you say. But at the right time, and in the right place," said Derek rather stiffly. "Now let's get on."

Jack picked up his folder from the floor, and

put it on Derek's desk. "Here's the report on my visit to the Cluck Cluck Diner. I'm afraid the list of staff and their details is incomplete. There's a lot of information missing. Larry Cluck Cluck isn't very good at keeping records."

"That's not a surprise," said Stanley. "I'm quite sure he's employing a few illegal immigrants. Beastly Boris for one."

"I did much better at Chez Les Chats, Sarge. Fearsome Frenchie keeps great records. I've asked Marmaduke to put the two lists through the computer to see what he can come up with."

"Well done, Jack. I'll give you the lists we got from the skating rink and the Cat-Odeon. You can give those to him at the same time. We also got a list of members from the skating rink. So there'll be squintillions of names for him to feed into the computer. Did you see Gloria when you were at Chez Les Chats, Jack?"

"As a matter of fact I did." Jack looked sheepish.

"And?"

"And what?"

"What happened? Did you ask her out on a date?"

Jack turned his head away, embarrassed.

"Come on, spill the beans," Stanley demanded.

"Well if you must know, we're going out to dinner tonight."

"*Miiiiiii .... aow*! What a result!" Stanley was really happy for his young colleague, and gave him an affectionate hug.

"Ahem!" coughed Derek. "Can we get back to cat-police business, please? I'm sorry about this, Jack, but I've got another assignment for you, and it needs to be taken care of immediately. So you'll have to postpone your date." Derek scribbled a note on a piece of paper. "I want you to go to this address and follow this cat." He showed Jack a rather tattered black and white photograph of Klepto Klaws. "I know it's not a very good photo, but it'll have to do. Anyway, he lives there on his own, so it shouldn't be too difficult. Take Pamela with you. I want you both to follow him wherever he goes. If you have to stay there all night, so be it."

Jack's face was a picture of disappointment, but like the good police-cat he was, he tried to keep his personal emotions in check. "What's the story, chief?"

It was Stanley who answered. "I'm hoping he'll lead you to a lock-up or a garage or something. We've had our eye on him for some time. We know he's fencing stolen goods, but so far we haven't been able to prove anything. I've got a fancy he might have Diamond Lil's necklace. And I'd like to get my hands on it before he sells it."

"So what do you want me to do if he leads me to some lock-up or other?"

"I want you to call me on your mobile, and give me the address. Then I want you to follow him again. Stick to him like glue, Jack."

"Try this one, Sarge," said Jack. "What's brown and sticky?"

Stanley shook his head.

"A stick!" shouted Jack. "Ha! Ha! Ha! I thought you'd have got that one, Sarge!"

"Ahem! Ahem! Ahem!" coughed Derek again. But he said nothing.

Jack just grinned.

"Leave Pamela to guard the lock-up," said Stanley, "till the Chief and I get there. Keep the office aware of your movements and we'll send you back up. If Klepto meets with anyone I want you to jump in straightaway and arrest them."

"That might be a bit difficult if I'm on my own, Sarge."

"I know. That's why we'll send you some back up."

There was a knock at the door.

"Come in," said Chief Inspector Dimwit.

Marmalade Marmaduke entered with a slice of toast and marmalade in his paw. "Good morning, Chief," he said before stuffing the toast into his mouth.

Derek shook his head in annoyance. "I suppose we've got to wait now while you finish what's in your mouth? Do you have to eat in cat-police time?"

"I get hungry in cat-police time," said Marmaduke, opening his mouth so that everyone could see its contents.

"Please, Marmaduke, mind your manners," said Stanley. "You should be more considerate of others. I remember what my old grandmother always used to say.

With your mouth full you should not speak.
Don't ever think that it's OK.
For if you do it every day,
You'll end up looking like a geek!"

Stanley winked at Jack.

Derek became agitated. "Why are you always eating toast and m-m-m-m-m-m....marmalade anyway? Why can't you eat toast and jam or toast and p-p-p-p-p-p....peanut butter for a change?"

"Well, I'd have to change my name wouldn't I? And that would confuse everyone. Anyway I've finished eating."

"What have you got?" asked Derek.

"We've had a phone call from a member of the cat-public. There's been a sighting of Beastly Boris."

Derek sat bolt upright. "Well why didn't you say so?"

"You're not going to like this, Chief. He was seen boarding an EasyCat flight at Catwick airport."

"G-g-g-g-g-goodness g-g-g-g-g-gracious!"

"Jumping Jellybeans!" said Jack.

"Do we know where he was flying to?" asked Stanley.

"We think it was Malaga, in the south of Spain."

Derek wrung his paws in frustration. "We've lost him. Our only suspect, and he's left the country. C-c-c-c-c-c....curses! This investigation isn't going well. Even a blind cat with a wooden leg can see that."

Tuesday 11th July

It was three o'clock in the afternoon when Jumping Jack and Playful Pamela pulled up opposite Klepto Klaws' house at the top of the hill. They were driving an unmarked silver grey Ford Mondeo from the motor pool.

"Would you like a coffee?" Pamela asked.

Jack nodded. Pamela unscrewed the top of the flask and poured two cups of strong, sweet, black coffee.

"I wonder how long we'll have to wait?" said Jack gloomily.

"You don't seem very happy, Jack."

"It's just that I had something planned for this evening."

"I know. I heard. It's a shame."

"You heard what?"

"That you had a hot date for tonight." Pamela grinned.

"How did you know?"

"Stanley told me. Said you might be a bit sore about it."

"Yeah well, I am."

"Don't upset yourself, Jack. You'll get another chance."

They lapsed into silence. Before long Pamela had fallen asleep, her gentle snoring fracturing the silence. Jack let her sleep, although he was wide-awake himself, thinking about Gloria and his missed opportunity. Lost in his own thoughts, Jack had no idea how long they had been waiting when he was alerted by a sudden whirring noise. He dug his paw into Pamela's ribs. When she opened her eyes he pointed across the street. The electric garage door was opening. A brand spanking new Mercedes Sports car reversed slowly and silently out of the garage. Klepto Klaws pointed the remote control and the door began to close.

Pamela was wide-awake now as Jack selected first gear. He pulled away from the kerb and followed the Mercedes, keeping a discreet distance between the two cars. Klepto's Mercedes went down the steep hill towards the town. It passed the cat-police station, went through the town centre, and over the level crossing. Turning right at the sea front, the Mercedes hugged the coastline road, driving on past the harbour, and began to leave the town behind. After about two kilometres it turned into an industrial estate, and Pamela put a restraining paw on Jack's elbow.

"We'd better stay well behind," she said. "He could lead us into a cul-de-sac. And then we'd be seen."

Jack nodded his agreement, and when the Mercedes made a right turn, Jack drove straight ahead. As they passed the turning the Mercedes had taken, Pamela was able to see that it had parked in front of a warehouse. The sign on the side of the building announced in large, bold letters …. West Industrial Air-Conditioning.

Fifty yards past the turning Jack pulled up. After a few minutes of thought he turned the vehicle round to face the direction they had come from. He would be ready to follow Klepto Klaws when he left the industrial estate. "You go round the corner and see what you can find out, Pam. If he comes out suddenly I'll follow him as agreed, and you can wait for Stanley. I'll call in now and let them know where we are."

Pamela got out of the car and walked towards the turning. As she reached the corner she stopped and bent down as if to tie a shoelace. Jack was already on the phone to the office when he saw the Mercedes ease out of the turning. He switched on the ignition.

"He's on the move already," he said to Cheerful Charlie back at the station. "He certainly didn't spend much time there. He *must* have gone in there to collect something. I'm following. Got to go, Charlie. Over and out."

They drove along the coast road, beyond the harbour and back towards the town centre. Jack was taken by surprise when Klepto Klaws turned into the slip road outside the Cat-Odeon, and took one of the half dozen parking spaces. For a moment or two he couldn't make up his mind what to do. He thought that he might be too exposed if he were to follow Klepto Klaws into the parking area. So he drove straight on. Immediately he regretted his decision. What if Klepto Klaws was not going to the cinema? Jack pulled up on the double yellow lines two hundred metres further on. He looked back to see Klepto Klaws walk past the Cat-Odeon and then on towards the sea.

Jack turned his car round and drove back to the Cat-Odeon and parked two spaces away from the Mercedes. He knew that there were only two likely places that Klepto Klaws would have gone. He went first into the pub that was next to the cinema, but there was no sign of Klepto. He walked towards the promenade, which ran parallel to the coast road alongside the beach.

The Sea View Café was at the rear of the cinema complex, attached to it at first floor level, but jutting out over the promenade almost as far as the sea wall. Jack knew that he would have to climb the wide stone steps to the café before he could be sure that Klepto Klaws was inside. He took out his mobile phone and called the station.

"Hello!" said a familiar voice. "Cat-Haven Cat-Police. Cheerful Charlie speaking. How can I help you?"

Jack gave Charlie a brief summary of what had occurred. "If I don't ring you back within five minutes, you can take it that Klepto Klaws *is* in the restaurant, and I'm watching him. Send down a back up unit fast – I'll need at least two cats. I'm pretty sure he's got some kind of package with him, and I'd rather not tackle him alone. Thanks Charlie."

Jack climbed the stairs and entered the restaurant. He saw Klepto Klaws straightaway, sitting at a window table overlooking the sea. He chose to sit in the opposite corner, which gave him a good view of Klepto. The waitress-cat, a silver blue Korat with luminous olive green eyes, came over to take Jack's order.

"I'll just have an orange juice, thank you." As soon as the words were out of his mouth he realised to his horror that he had no money or credit cards with him. But it was too late. He was committed to keeping Klepto Klaws under observation.

Rain was falling steadily, the wind lashing against the windows. Jack gazed out at the beach below. It was deserted, save for a lone seagull that was strutting along the sand. It dipped its feet in the sea, allowing the gentle ripples of the outgoing tide to lap round its ankles. It seemed to be looking out towards the horizon where a large ship was anchored a kilometre or two out to sea. A large cat, muffled up against the weather, came in to view. He was strolling along the beach with his dog. The summer months were for the tourist-cats, and locals were not allowed to walk their dogs on the beach. Jack guessed that if Chief Inspector Dimwit had been with him, he would probably have gone down to the beach and arrested the cat on the spot. He smiled to himself at the thought.

He saw the waitress-cat approaching Klepto's table. She placed a plate of sausages, beans and chips in front of him. "What the hell is this?" shouted Klepto. "I didn't order this!"

"Yes you did." The look that the waitress-cat gave Klepto told Jack that she would not back down.

"No I didn't. I don't like sausages." Klepto's tone was extremely unpleasant.

"You did order it, you potty old crock!"

Klepto cupped a furry paw round the back of one of his comically large ears. "What did you say?"

"You heard! With ears as big as that you couldn't fail to hear!"

Klepto Klaws glared at her. "You're an insolent little cow. Dump this and give me what I ordered." He pushed the plate away.

"I'll give you what you ordered, sir." The waitress-cat's voice was as cold as Arctic ice. Calmly she picked up the plate. "And as requested I'll dump it." She tipped up the plate and deposited the entire contents into Klepto's lap. And for good measure she picked up his mug of hot, steaming tea, and poured it on top of the sausages, beans and chips. Klepto screamed. The waitress-cat swished her head dramatically and walked away from the table.

Jack was watching this drama unfold with some amusement, but his eyes narrowed sharply when he saw Klepto Klaws hurriedly take a small package from his trouser pocket and place it on the table. It was something wrapped in white tissue paper, and appeared to have been stained by the hot tea that had leaked through his trousers.

"I bet that's the necklace," Jack muttered under his breath. He thought of racing across the restaurant and snatching the package from the table. But before he had made a decision he saw a tall, smartly dressed cat, a Lilac Silver Shaded Burmilla, walk briskly into the restaurant. Klepto Klaws' struggled to rise from his chair, brushing sausage and beans from his trousers onto the floor. The contrast between the two cats was comical, thought Jack. On the one hand was an ugly cat whose clothes were soggy and stained with food, and on the other a good looking cat dressed in a crisp, freshly laundered white shirt and well pressed blue trousers.

Jack leaned forward, straining to overhear what they were saying. But he was unable to pick up more than an occasional word. At the end of a brief conversation the smartly dressed Burmilla handed Klepto a brown envelope. He then picked up the stained package and strode out of the restaurant.

Jack was taken aback by how swiftly all this had occurred. He had no time to consider what he should do next. Without giving the matter any real thought, he decided to follow the package. Fortunately the waitress-cat was too busy complaining to her colleague to notice that Jack was leaving the restaurant without paying.

Tuesday 11th July

Pamela greeted Stanley and Derek when they arrived at the air-conditioning warehouse. Marmaduke and Tammy were with them and the rain was teeming down. Access to the warehouse was by way of a large wooden door, which was securely locked. Stanley opened the boot of the car and took out an axe. He handed it to Marmaduke, who looked at it uncertainly. "Break the door down, lad," said Stanley encouragingly.

Marmaduke hefted the axe over his shoulder, and as he began to swing it towards the door he slipped on the wet ground and pitched forward. Stanley put out a paw to try and save him from falling. But it was too late. With an almighty thwack Marmaduke's head smashed into the wooden door, and the axe struck nothing more than fresh air. He fell to the ground, reeling from the blow to his head. Stanley knelt down, concerned for his young colleague.

Marmaduke looked up. "Sorry, Sarge, that was a bit of a shambles!"

"Are you all right, Marmy?"

"I'm fine," said Marmaduke trying to be brave.

"Would you like a glass of water?" asked Derek.

"I know what I would like, Chief, and that's a slice of toast and marmalade."

"That's a bit difficult right now. Perhaps you ought to go and sit in the car for a while."

"No, I'll be all right. Let me have another go, Sarge."

Stanley had already picked up the axe. "Leave it to me, Marmaduke." It took no time at all to break the door open. Pamela was left to stand guard outside, in case Klepto Klaws made an unexpected appearance.

Inside the building they were confronted by rows and rows of shelving, full of boxes. "I don't suppose there'll be anything to interest us here," said Stanley. "Let's see if we can find an office, or a storeroom."

They found an office at the rear of the building. It was locked. Stanley put his shoulder to it, and the lock gave way immediately. The office was oddly out of keeping with the industrial surroundings. There were two large, expensive-looking, black leather settees, each with a glass table in front of it, and a curved desk with a black leather swivel chair behind it. Stanley made straight for the landscape painting behind the desk, and took it down from the wall. And there, set into the brick, was a combination safe.

"Do you want me to try and break into it, Sarge?" asked Marmaduke.

"Not for the moment, Marmy. Let's see where this door takes us." He led the way through a door that opened into a large storeroom.

"Good heavens," said Stanley, "it's a treasure trove. There's squintillions of stuff!" There were shelves round three sides of the room, from floor to ceiling. They were crammed with objects of all descriptions. There were several boxes full of clocks and watches, and others with teddy bears and cuddly toys. There were tennis rackets and golf clubs, television sets and radios, leather wallets and handbags, and paintings of all shapes and sizes. "Look here, Stan," said Derek. "Boxes with radiators in them!"

Stanley nodded. "This is a whole lot better than a slap in the eye with a wet fish. We've got enough here to put Klepto Klaws behind bars for years and years."

"Do you think we should get on to the office, Stan, and get them to send some cat-constables to arrest Klepto and take him back to the station?"

"Just what I was going to suggest, Chief. I also think we should get another two cats to come here and make a complete list of all the items in this storeroom. I bet most of it turns out to be stolen property. Marmy, get on to the station and ask Charlie to organise it. Tell him we want two cars to come here. You, Tammy and Pamela can wait here till they arrive, and then take the second car back to the station. We also need an expert to get the safe open – ask Charlie to get someone from Emergency Cat-Locksmiths down here right away."

"I'll get on to it straightaway, Sarge."

"Good. As soon as that's organised you and I can go back to the station, Chief, and await the arrival of our friend Klepto Klaws."

Derek led the way back into the office and he was unable to believe his eyes. Tammy Tickletummy was lying on top of the desk, on her back, with her paws in the air, fast asleep!

"What *are* you doing, Tammy?" he shouted.

Tammy awoke with a start. "What?" she said sleepily.

"What on earth are you doing?"

"Oh, it's you, Chief. I was just having a catnap. Sorry, but I just had to have a rest. As you know I'm a growing cat, and I'm hungry again. And when I know I'm going to have to wait a while before my next meal, I need to have a sleep in order to take my mind off my hunger. It's inconvenient I know, but my mammy has always drummed it into me that you need to eat to keep up your energy levels. And if your energy levels are low, you need to sleep."

"You're going to get the sack, Tammy, if you don't buck your ideas up."

"That's so unfair. If you sack me for enjoying my basic cat rights in the workplace, Chief, I'll take you and the Cat-Haven Cat-Police to the industrial cat-tribunal."

Derek was shocked into silence.

"I wonder how Jack's getting on," said Stanley.

When Jack hurried out of the restaurant and took the stairs down to the street, he saw the Burmilla walking along the sea front promenade towards the harbour, sheltering under an umbrella. The rain was falling steadily, and Jack accepted the fact that he was going to get pretty wet. He followed carefully, making sure that he wasn't seen. To his surprise the Burmilla turned into Cod Place, and approached the Fish Market. Jack could not understand this at all, since the Fish Market was closed. It was only when the Burmilla entered the car park that Jack realised that this was where he had parked his car. Jack saw him climb into a Jaguar motor car and prepare to drive off. His own car was still outside the Cat-Odeon, and he knew that his only hope of maintaining contact was to find a taxi. He ran as fast as he could back towards the coast road. His luck was in. Just as the Jaguar was about to emerge from Cod Place Jack spotted a taxi coming towards him. He jumped in and flashed his warrant card at the driver.

"Cat-Haven Cat-Police," he said. "Follow that car."

The taxi driver was a Seal Mitted Blue Snowshoe wearing a Cat-Haven Gooners red baseball cap. "Right ho, Guv," he said enthusiastically. "I've always wanted to be asked by a copper to 'follow that car'. Just like in the movies, eh?"

The Jaguar glided along the coast road for several kilometres, and eventually turned into Cat-Haven Point apartment block.

Jack instructed the driver to pull up close to the entrance, and pretended he was searching his pockets for money. But he was fully alert and watchful. The Burmilla got out of the Jaguar and walked towards the apartment building. Would he use a key? Or would he buzz one of the apartments? Jack clearly saw him press the top button and speak rapidly into the intercom for a few seconds. The door was buzzed open for him.

Jack waited for a full minute before getting out of the taxi. He went up to the intercom panel. There were seventeen buttons. Next to each of the buttons numbered one to sixteen was the name of the cat who lived there. The top button however, simply carried the word Penthouse. Satisfied, Jack went back to the taxi. "I'm going to have to ask you to wait here for the time being," he said to the driver. Although it was still raining heavily, Jack knew that he couldn't telephone the station from the cab. He didn't want to be overheard. He walked back towards the apartment block, which afforded a certain amount of shelter from the rain, and dialled the station on his mobile.

"Hello Charlie. It's me again, Jack. I need you to re-route the back up team. Klepto Klaws passed a package to a Burmilla in the restaurant. I can't explain why, but I think the package contains the diamond necklace. Anyway, I followed the Burmilla, and at the moment he's inside an apartment block on the sea front. I think he's visiting somebody. I'm standing outside the apartment block. Who are in the back up team by the way?"

"Soppy Cynthia and Studious Stephen."

"Dear oh dear! Not exactly the best cats for this sort of operation."

"I know, Jack. Sorry about that, but they were the only two cats available. Which apartment block is it?"

"Cat-Haven Point."

"That's interesting. That's where Miss Ping Pong lives. Any idea which apartment number the suspect is visiting?"

"The penthouse."

There was a sharp intake of breath before Charlie continued. "That's Miss Ping Pong's apartment."

"Jumping Jellybeans!"

"Exactly! Right, I'll get the back up to you straightaway. I'm going to let the Chief know about this. I'm sure he'll come straight over. I suggest you do nothing until he arrives."

"What if the Burmilla comes out?"

"In that case you'll have to arrest him. Let's hope it doesn't come to that. Let's hope the Chief gets there in time."

****

Derek Dimwit was stunned by Cheerful Charlie's call. He told Stanley of this startling development as they were leaving the air-conditioning warehouse.

"That's not good news, Derek," said Stanley sympathetically.

"I can't believe Ping Pong is mixed up in something like this, Stanley. It's c-c-c-c-c-c.......completely out of character! I have to deal with this myself. Charlie knew I'd want to, and he's instructed Jack to do nothing until we get there."

When the Panda car with Cynthia and Stephen on board pulled up outside the apartment block, Jack ran over to the car. Cynthia was at the wheel. This surprised Jack, since he knew that she had only passed her cat-driving test last week. When he saw that Stephen had his head buried in a book, he knew why Cynthia was driving.

"Put that book away, Stephen," said Jack. "There's no time for reading when we're on a field operation. Have you got any money with you?"

Stephen looked a bit put out. "Yes, I have."

"Good. Go and pay the taxi driver."

"Hello, Jack," said Cynthia nervously. "I've never been on an operation before. Will it be dangerous?"

"Of course not, Cyn. Don't worry. We've got nothing to do at the moment. You'll be all right." He climbed into the passenger seat and patted her on the knee.

Soppy Cynthia was the newest cadet-cat on the Cat-Haven Cat-Police force. She was a red Spotted Tabby Munchkin with short legs and a short tail. She looked a bit like a squirrel when she sat up on her haunches with her paws off the ground, and all the other cats laughed at her. In truth she did look rather comical, but Jack thought it really unfair that the other cadet-cats were so cruel to her. They'd changed her name from Ginger to Soppy Cynthia on her second day at the station, mostly because she seemed helpless and made stupid mistakes. Only Jack, Marmaduke and Stanley had been kind to her.

She looked adoringly at Jack. "Thank you, Jack," she said.

"We're waiting for Chief Inspector Dimwit."

No sooner had he uttered these words than a cat-police panda car came screaming up to the apartment block. Derek jumped out, closely followed by Stanley. Jack was already getting out of the other panda car.

"Are you sure the suspect went to the penthouse, Jack?" said Derek.

"Well, I didn't actually see him enter the penthouse, but he definitely buzzed the penthouse button."

Derek went straight over to the front door and buzzed up.

Ping Pong could see that it was Derek on the video intercom. "Doody!" she squealed. "It's you! What a lovely surprise. Come on up."

The door buzzed and Derek pushed it open. "Stanley, you and Jack come with me. You others stay here and wait."

The elevator took them to the top floor. The door opened directly into the penthouse apartment. Ping Pong had a broad smile on her face, but it disappeared as soon as she saw that Derek was not alone.

"I'm sorry, Ping Pong, but this is an official visit." Derek pointed to Ping Pong's throat. "Where did you get that necklace?"

Ping Pong was taken aback. "That's not a very nice way to ask. In fact it's not a very nice question."

"Don't make this difficult, Ping Pong. You know I have my job to do, and I need to know where you got that necklace."

"My brother gave it to me."

"Your brother?"

"Yes, my brother."

"When did he give it to you?"

"Ten minutes ago."

"Where is he now?"

"Derek, why are you treating me like this? Anyone would think I was a criminal."

"I'm sorry, Ping Pong. But I have to get to the bottom of this. Do you mean your brother Sing Song?"

Ping Pong didn't answer.

"Where is he now?"

"He left a couple of minutes ago."

"Did he leave by the stairs?"

"Yes. Just after I told him you were coming up."

"Jack," said Stanley, "take the stairs over there, and catch him. And when you do, arrest him."

Jack set off at a run.

"What do you mean, arrest him?" Ping Pong started to cry.

"Give me that necklace, Ping Pong," said Derek. "I have reason to believe that it's stolen property."

"Stolen property? It can't be."

"Ping Pong, just give it to me."

"Are you trying to suggest that my brother is a thief?"

Derek said nothing, and just held out his paw.

Ping Pong wiped her eyes, and undid the necklace. Her manner changed abruptly. "You'll regret this, Derek." She spat out the words venomously.

Derek was shocked by Ping Pong's outburst, and cursed himself for not handling the situation better. He took the necklace and handed it to Stanley. "We'll give you a receipt for it, Ping Pong. It goes without saying that if it turns out that it's not stolen, you'll get it back. I'm just doing my duty."

"I suppose that makes it all right, does it?"

"I'm doing my best in a difficult situation, Ping Pong. I *am* a cat-police officer, you know."

"How could I forget it. Now go to hell! If you've finished, you can leave my apartment." She turned her back on Derek, and stalked into the kitchen, slamming the door behind her.

Derek was lost for words.

Stanley reached out and touched Derek on the shoulder.

"Come, Chief," he said gently, "let's go back to the station and see if Klepto Klaws is already in custody."

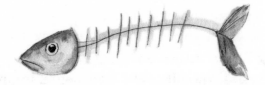

Tuesday 11th July

Klepto Klaws was dragged into the station in pawcuffs. He was not a happy cat. Marmaduke took hold of his elbow. "Get your filthy paws off me," screamed Klepto.

Just then Greta the Grumbler appeared in the doorway. "I suppose you all want a cup of tea now, don't you?" she said.

"I'll have one," said Klepto rudely. "Milk and two sugars."

"Sorry," said Cheerful Charlie, "the rule book says no tea for suspects. Not until they've told us all we want to know. Take him to the interview room, Cat-Constable Marmaduke, and empty his pockets."

Klepto was left on his own for the best part of an hour before any other cat entered the interview room. Stanley and Derek went in together. Stanley sat down at the table opposite Klepto Klaws, but deliberately he did not look at him directly. He made no eye contact. Derek stood behind Klepto.

Stanley picked up the microphone and turned on the tape recorder. "This is Sergeant Stanley Smartpants of Cat-Haven Cat-Police conducting an interview with Mr Klepto Klaws at ...." Stanley paused to check the clock on the wall. "...... 9.13 p.m. on Tuesday 11th July 2008. Also present is Chief Inspector Derek Dimwit." He switched the tape off, and leaned across the table, his face only millimetres away from Klepto's, and looked directly into his eyes. "I promise you, Klepto, you'll tell us what we want to know. And quickly. This will be a very short interview, then Chief Inspector Dimwit and I are going home. If you haven't told us what we want to know you'll just have to spend the night in one of the cells. So it would pay you to cooperate." Stanley turned the tape back on.

"I want to take you back to our meeting yesterday. We talked about a diamond necklace that was stolen from Cat-Diamonds "R" Us. Are you ready to admit that you bought it from the cat who stole it?"

"Of course not. I've already told you, I know nothing about it."

"Who did you buy it from, Klepto?"

"Nobody."

"You must have bought it from somebody," said Derek from over Klepto's shoulder.

Klepto twisted round in his seat to face Derek.

"Don't try and trick me into admitting something. I've told you, I don't know anything about the necklace."

"When I mentioned the diamond necklace to you yesterday, your exact words were ...." Stanley paused to take out his notebook .... "and for the record I am quoting the notes I made at the meeting just referred to .... yes, I read about it in the Cat-Haven Chronicle."

Klepto twisted back and looked Stanley square in the eye. "So what," he said unpleasantly

"Do you stand by that?"

"Yes."

"Do you stand by that?" repeated Derek. "And look at me when I'm talking to you."

Klepto refused to acknowledge this remark and stared straight ahead.

"Chief, would you show Klepto that copy of the Cat-Haven Chronicle?"

"For the record," said Derek, "we are looking at the front page of the Cat-Haven Chronicle dated Monday 10th July. Please read this, Klepto." Klepto Klaws was forced to turn back to Derek, and he scanned the page of newsprint briefly.

"As you can see," continued Stanley, "there is no mention of a diamond necklace, either on the front page or anywhere else in the newspaper."

Klepto Klaws said nothing.

"How did you know about the necklace, Klepto?"

"I didn't."

"Isn't it true that you *did* know about it?" said Derek.

"Yesterday you admitted that you did," said Stanley.

"No I didn't. *You* mentioned the robbery at Cat-Diamonds "R" Us, and that *was* in the paper. *You were the one* who said that the necklace came from the Cat-Diamonds "R" Us store. I just put two and two together. The fact that the necklace *wasn't* mentioned in the paper is irrelevant. You were just trying to trick me."

"You were seen with the necklace no more than a couple of hours ago."

"That's nonsense."

Derek interrupted. "You were seen in a restaurant on the sea front."

Klepto became agitated. "So what! I probably went there to eat."

"Don't play cat and mouse with us," said Stanley. "You were seen with the necklace. It was wrapped in white tissue paper."

Klepto Klaws said nothing, but his body language encouraged Stanley to think that their tactics were paying off.

"Do you deny that you had a package wrapped in white tissue paper?"

"If for the sake of argument I *did* have a package wrapped in tissue paper, how on earth could you know what it contained?"

Derek interrupted once more, and repeated Stanley's previous question. "Do you deny that you had a package wrapped in white tissue paper?"

"I don't have to answer your questions."

"I wouldn't be aggressive if I were you, Klepto," said Stanley.

Klepto smiled crookedly. "I'm not being aggressive, Sergeant. I'm just making you aware of my rights."

"It doesn't matter, Klepto. We have a witness."

"A witness to what?" Klepto's tone was scornful.

"You'll find out soon enough," said Derek.

Stanley picked up the internal telephone. "Charlie, bring in the witness please." He looked directly into Klepto's eyes, and momentarily he thought he saw a flash of apprehension. There was a light knock on the door, and in walked Jack. "For the record," said Stanley for the benefit of the tape recording, "Cat-Constable Jumping Jack has just entered the room. Jack, can you please confirm that this was the cat you saw in the sea front restaurant."

Jack crossed the room and stood at Stanley's side. He stared hard at Klepto. "This is definitely the cat, Sergeant," said Jack simply.

"And can you also confirm that you saw this cat pass a package wrapped in white tissue paper to a silver-white Burmilla, who was wearing blue trousers?"

"I can."

"Thank you, Jack, that will be all for the moment."

Jack left the interview room.

"What do you have to say now, Klepto?" said Derek.

Klepto turned round. "It proves nothing."

Stanley switched the point of attack. "I also asked you yesterday," he said harshly, "about some stolen radiators. Do you remember?"

Klepto was silent.

"Of course you do, and you told me that you knew nothing about them. That being the case, how do you explain the fact that we found a quantity of radiators in your air-conditioning warehouse earlier this evening?"

Stanley reached under the desk and pushed a button.

"I want to show you something, Klepto." A panel in the wall slid back to reveal a two-way glass mirror that enabled them to see into the adjoining room. Sing Song was pacing up and down, looking decidedly uncomfortable.

"For the record," said Derek, "we are now looking through the two-way mirror into the adjoining interview room."

It was Stanley's turn. "As you well know, Klepto, the cat in the adjoining room is your contact, Sing Song."

"And he's sung quite a song for us," said Derek. "Quite a song!"

Klepto was stunned. Stanley noted that his eyes

widened, a sure sign that he was frightened. His tough guy image had melted away, like a puff of smoke in the wind.

"For the record, I have taken out of my pocket a diamond necklace, and I am placing it on the table. We believe it to be the necklace stolen from Cat-Diamonds "R" Us four days ago. What do you have to say now, Klepto?"

Klepto was badly shaken, but he composed himself before speaking. "I'm not prepared to answer any more questions, unless my lawyer is present."

"You can of course refuse to answer any more questions until your solicitor arrives," said Derek. "That is your right as a citizen-cat."

"And obviously that won't be tonight," said Stanley. "You'll have to spend the night in the cells. Do you wish to say anything else?"

"No."

"This interview is terminated at 9.31 p.m.," said Stanley. He turned off the tape recorder.

Wednesday 12th July

"Look here, Sing Song," said Chief Inspector Dimwit, "as I've already said, Ping Pong told us that you gave her the necklace."

"If you think she'll agree to say that, you're mistaken," replied Sing Song.

On this occasion the cat-police roles were reversed. Derek was sitting at the table opposite the suspect, and Stanley had taken up a position behind Sing Song.

"I don't want to have to drag Ping Pong into court to give evidence against you."

"I'll bet you don't. It would finish your relationship with her. Anyway, she won't give evidence against her brother."

"It's not wise of you to threaten the Chief of the Cat-Police, Sing Song," said Stanley. "But we'll let that pass." Sing Song twisted round in his chair to look at Stanley. "I don't think you realise the seriousness of your position. You've been caught red-pawed receiving stolen property. And despite your denials it's as plain as the whiskers on your face that you knew the necklace was stolen."

"Even a blind cat with a wooden leg, could see that," said Derek.

"Come on, Sing Song," continued Stanley, "everyone knows that you buy expensive jewellery in a jewellery store, not in a fish and chip café. This necklace is worth ten thousand cat-euros. It's just not believable that you bought it legally in a fish and chip restaurant!"

"I've done nothing wrong."

It was Derek's turn. "And of course you didn't pay 10,000 cat-euros for it, did you? I suppose you bought it for a song!" Stanley had great difficulty keeping a straight face, but Derek seemed not to notice and ploughed on. "How do you know Klepto Klaws?"

"I've never heard of him. Who is he?"

Stanley spoke next. "He's the cat you bought the necklace from, Sing Song. As we've already told you, we have a witness who saw you hand Klepto Klaws a brown envelope in exchange for a small package wrapped in white tissue paper. We found that tissue paper, complete with tea stains, in Ping Pong's apartment. And no doubt the envelope you gave to Klepto Klaws contained cash. How much did you pay for the necklace?"

"I've done nothing wrong," repeated Sing Song.

"We'll be the judge of that." With that Derek reached under the desk and pressed a button. The partition slid back to reveal the two-way mirror. Sing Song visibly blanched when he saw Klepto Klaws in the next room.

"We're going to level with you, Sing Song," said Stanley. "In this particular matter it's Klepto Klaws we're after. We know he handles stolen property, and then sells it on to gullible cats like you. If you cooperate with us, help us to nail Klepto Klaws, we'll consider dropping any charges against you."

"We're going to leave you for a few minutes to think it over," said Derek. He turned off the tape machine, and he and Stanley left the interview room.

They left Sing Song considering his position. Stanley went up to his office and sat at his desk. He turned on the monitor that picked up the pictures from the camera situated in the interview room. He was able to observe Sing Song closely. He was a cat with a lot on his mind, thought Stanley. Every now and then he glanced at Klepto Klaws on the other side of the two way mirror. He had a nervous tic at the corner of his left eye, and he was swishing his tail back and forth. He looked scared out of his wits, and he started to pace up and down. Stanley smiled to himself. His instinct told him that it would not be long before Sing Song was ready to talk.

****

They left him alone for half an hour.

"Well," said Derek when they returned. "Do you have anything to tell us, Sing Song?"

"Let's say I did buy the necklace," said Sing Song slowly. "If I did, I bought it for my sister in good faith. How was I supposed to know it was stolen?"

"How much did you pay for it?" asked Stanley.

Sing Song thought long and hard before turning round and speaking to Stanley. "Four thousand cat-euros," he said finally.

"Now we're getting somewhere." Stanley picked up the internal telephone. "Greta," he said, "can you please bring in three cups of tea, and your notepad. Mr Sing Song is going to sing us a sweet song."

An hour later Sing Song was released without charge. Derek Dimwit was pleased that it had not taken too long to get his confession. He wasn't sure if they had done the right thing in not charging him with receiving stolen property. But at least it gave him an outside chance of repairing his relationship with Ping Pong. Although Klepto Klaws was still refusing to answer questions, they felt sure that they had enough evidence against him to charge him with receiving the stolen necklace.

Derek and Stanley took the panda car to Cat-Diamonds "R" Us. They found Diamond Lil in her office being comforted by Pretty Peaches. Lil's face was puffy and she looked exhausted. It was clear that she had been crying some more.

"Put those tissues away, Lil," said Stanley. "we've found the necklace! At least we're pretty sure it's your necklace, although we need you to confirm it." He put his hand into the pocket of his pink and grey striped trousers, took out the necklace and handed it to Lil.

Lil was overcome with joy and burst into tears. But they were tears of happiness. "Yes, yes, it's my necklace! Oh, Stan, you're a genius-cat!" She rushed up to him and threw her paws around him. She smothered him with kisses. Stanley was embarrassed at Lil's display of affection in front of Peaches. Meanwhile Derek looked on enviously.

"We must celebrate," said Lil. "I always keep a couple of bottles of champagne in my office fridge, you know, for wealthy clients. Peaches, would you like to get a bottle out while I get the glasses. Oh, happy day!"

"Awesome!" exclaimed Peaches and nearly fell over herself in her rush to get to the fridge.

"That is soooo cool, Lil," said Stanley

"I'm not sure," said Derek. "We shouldn't really drink champagne. After all we *are* on duty."

"Just one glass won't hurt, Chief. It's a really special occasion."

"I hear what you say, Stan ………… and I approve!" Derek grinned.

Peaches pulled out the champagne cork with a

loud pop, and the sparkling liquid fizzed over the top of the bottle and onto her paws. "Wow!" she said, and passed the bottle to Lil.

Lil poured champagne into the four glasses. "A toast! To Stanley and Chief Inspector Dimwit."

"Lil, please call me Derek."

Lil smiled. "Of course ..... Derek. Thank you both so much. If we had never seen the necklace again, I think I would probably have had to close the business down. So here's to you and the Cat-Haven cat-police force!"

Peaches gulped her champagne a bit too fast, and the fizzy bubbles went up her nose. She laughed and moved close to Stanley. She put her head on his shoulder and twisted round so that she was gazing into his eyes. "Ooooh! It goes straight to your head, doesn't it?" She laughed again.

The four cats sat and talked happily and drank their champagne. After about twenty minutes Stanley turned to his boss. "I think we'll have to make a move, Chief. We need to get back to the office. Lil, perhaps you could come up to the station sometime later to sign a statement to the effect that this is the necklace that was stolen. I'm terribly sorry, but I'll have to hang on to it for a little while. I'll need it for evidence."

Wednesday 12 July

"Hey Stan, how you doin'?" said Francesca as she walked into Stanley's office. "That's some outfit you're wearing!"

Stanley smiled. He was dressed from head to toe in yellow. He had a bright yellow t-shirt, beautifully tailored yellow trousers, yellow socks, and finally a pair of yellow shoes.

"A bit dangerous though, isn't it?"

Stanley looked puzzled. "How do you mean?"

"One of your own police-cats might attack you. I mean, you do look like a canary!"

"That was a …. *cheap* …. remark, Francesca!"

Francesca laughed. "Good response, Stan! OK, I've got something for you on the blue hairs found at the Skating Rink. They're a perfect match with the hairs found at Granny Garbo's and Cat-Diamonds "R" Us. And the same traces of garlic butter, shallots and white wine were present on the mackerel bones. All in all, we're confident that the same cat committed all three crimes." She spoke very precisely, as if she was giving evidence in court.

"Good news. Thanks, Francesca. Did you get a good image from the pawprint?"

"Yep, it's a good one. We checked it out against the database, but it doesn't match anything we've got."

"Only to be expected, I guess. At least it means we can discount any of the criminal-cats who are known to us. And what about the breed?"

"I'm sorry Stan, but we're not going to be able to come up with an answer on that. The equipment you have here just isn't sophisticated enough."

"Pliff!"

"There is a way though. We do have the right equipment in our lab in Catmel. If I could fly out to California and take the evidence with me, we'd come up with the breed in no time."

"Hmm, perhaps it *would* be a good idea. If only we knew the breed we'd be able to eliminate a lot of suspects."

"Do you have a lot of suspects, Stan?"

"Not exactly. But Marmaduke is preparing a detailed list of employees, regular visitor-cats, worker-cats and so on at the various crime scenes, and obviously any blue-haired cats are serious suspects."

There was a knock at the door, and Marmaduke entered munching a piece of toast and marmalade.

"Have you got a minute, Sarge?"

"I wish you wouldn't walk into my office eating toast, Marmaduke. Breadcrumbs all over the floor are an open invitation to mice."

Marmaduke chuckled. "You're havin' a laugh, Sarge. Mice shouldn't be a problem for a cop shop full of cats!"

"That's what *you* think! Most cats are hopeless at catching mice. I mean, how many times did Tom ever catch Jerry?"

"I thought you liked mice anyway. I seem to remember the last time a mouse turned up in the Crime Room, you got all google-eyed and soppy. 'Chuck, chuck, chuck, little fellow! Wasn't that it?" Marmaduke burst out laughing.

Stanley couldn't help but smile. "OK, Marmy, you win this time. Anyway, come in and sit down." He turned his attention back to Francesca. "I'll tell Chuck you're coming over, Fran. Ask Greta to check out flights on Cat-Virgin Atlantic from Heathcat in the next day or so."

"I've come up with something interesting," said Marmaduke. "I haven't finished putting all the employee lists through the computer yet, but I have made an interesting discovery. I've come across a Russian Blue. His name is Vladimir Katakov."

"Now that *is* interesting. Where did you find him?"

"He's a handycat at the Cat-Odeon. And he's definitely Russian. Perhaps he's related to Beastly

Boris."

"Yuri and Vladimir Katakov! Every chance they're related, I'd say. It's not exactly a common name, is it? Do we have his home address?"

"No. It's not in the file."

"Hmm. We've got *two* Katakovs in Cat-Haven, and both of them seem to be here illegally."

"I have got one more thing, Stan," said Francesca. "The piece of grey cotton found at Cat Diamonds "R" Us is from a pair of jeans that were made in China."

"Unfortunately that's not going to help us much. Squintillions of things are made in China these days!"

"I knew that would be a disappointment."

While Francesca returned to her laboratory, Stanley and Marmaduke went to the Crime Room. Jumping Jack was surrounded by a group of cat-constables and cadet-cats, telling them a story.

"There were these three French cats," he was saying, "and they were walking along a river bank in the South of France. They wanted to cross to the other side of the river. Eventually they came to a narrow, old and rickety wooden bridge. Although it looked pretty weak and wishy-washy, the three cats didn't hesitate, and stepped out onto it. It swayed alarmingly as they walked one behind the other, in single file. When they were about halfway across there was a sudden shattering noise as the bridge began to break up. The three French cats stood frozen in horror, unable to decide whether to run back where they had come from or race across to the other side. Too late! With a final screeching and tearing of broken wood, the bridge collapsed, and the three poor little creatures were hurled into the rushing water below." Jack paused for effect before continuing. "And ...*un...deux...trois... cat...sank!* Ha! Ha! Ha!"

The punch line was greeted with howls of laughter.

"Nice one, Jackster," said Marmaduke.

"Look, Pam," said Tammy, "Stephen doesn't get it. He doesn't speak French."

"Yes I do," said Stephen. "I just didn't find it very funny."

"Well I don't get it," said Cynthia. "Can someone explain it to me?"

"You are stupid, Cynthia," said Stephen. "That's how they count from one to five in French .... un, deux, trois, cat, sank. Got it?"

"Stop picking on her," said Pamela.

"Yes, leave her alone, Stephen," said Stanley. "Not all cats speak French. Anyway, sorry to break up the party, but we have a suspect to arrest."

"Is it Vladimir Katakov, Sarge?" asked Jack, all bright eyed. "When Marmaduke mentioned his name a few minutes ago I guessed you'd want to interview him."

"Yes, Jack. I'd like you and Marmaduke to follow that up. I suggest you go to the Cat-Odeon first to find out his working schedule. I don't want you to ask directly about him. I don't want to alert him to the fact that we're interested in him. Beastly Boris is still our prime suspect, remember. If Vladimir *is* related to Boris, he might have information that would be useful to us. I don't want *him* to disappear as well. Just make it a general inquiry. Tell Miserable Melvin that you want to build up a picture of their staff working patterns. Try and get a list of who's working when over the next week. That sort of thing. With a bit of luck you should be able to get a handle on Vladimir's movements. Then we can follow him after he finishes work, and find out where he lives. Report back to me when you've got the information. Then we'll arrest him."

The office phone rang on Jack's desk, and he picked it up. "It's for you, Sarge. It's Greta."

Stanley took the phone and put it to his ear. He listened intently, a deep furrow creasing his brow. "Have you told the Chief?" he asked. And after a pause, "OK tell him I'll meet him in his office in five minutes." He put down the phone. "There's been another robbery. At the Kitty Kat Ice Cream Parlour on the sea front. I think it's time we had an incident board with details of all the robbery locations, clues, evidence, suspects and so on. Marmaduke, I'd like you to organise that. When do you think you'll have completed the analysis from the employee files?"

"It should be finished later today Sarge, or at worst

by first thing tomorrow morning. I'll have an Incident Board up by the end of tomorrow."

Chief Inspector Dimwit checked the clock on the wall of his office. It was 6.00 p.m. Ping Pong should be at home. He dialled her number.

"Hello, Ping Pong, it's Derek."

Ping Pong said nothing. There was an uncomfortable silence, broken only by the sound of Ping Pong's heavy breathing.

"I've got good news for you. Sing Song has been most helpful in our inquiries. He's signed a statement, and left here a few hours ago."

"I know." There was a coldness in Ping Pong's voice that was rather worrying.

"I guess you must have spoken to him," said Derek rather pointlessly. "Did he tell you about the necklace?"

"Yes."

"I'm sorry, Ping Pong, but it *was* stolen. It's our duty to return it to its rightful owner.

"Fine. So you're just doing your duty, then?"

Derek couldn't think of anything to say.

"Fine," said Ping Pong once more. "Well if that's all, I've got things to do." She slammed down the receiver.

Derek was left with the noise of the phone line buzzing in his ear, and a queasy feeling in the pit of his stomach.

Thursday 13th July

The Kitty Kat Ice Cream Parlour was the most exciting place in the whole of Cat-Haven. It was the town's Number One tourist attraction. Cats and their kittens came from far and wide to sample its delights. It wasn't just an ice cream store. My goodness no! It was a fun palace for kittens and adult cats of all ages. **Forget Disneyland – come to Kitty Kat IceCreamland!** screamed their publicity.

It covered an entire block along the sea front. Its most celebrated feature was the fun and play area, known as Krazy Kitten Korner. Curiously it was slap bang in the middle of the store! The area was like an atrium, open to the skies, although there was a sliding roof which could be closed when it was raining or the weather was cold. There was a pool in the centre with two water slides. A giant one for older kittens, and a smaller one for kittens only a few weeks old. Kittens of all ages loved to play and splash and slide in the pool. It was such fun. Around the edges of the pool was a clear plastic splash guard "fence". This meant that the tables and chairs round the pool could remain dry. More importantly, parent-cats were shielded from being splashed, but still able to keep an eye on their kittens.

There were two four-sided Ice-Cream Fun Enclosures, one on either side of the pool. These were even more popular than the water slides. The **Delicious Ice-Cream Chamber** was an enclosed play area with clear plastic walls for maximum viewing fun. It had climbing frames and ramps, all leading up to a large platform. Above the platform, just out of reach, were rows of wafer cones filled with every variety of ice cream available. In order to reach the ice creams kittens had to leap off the platform. To make it more fun the ice cream cones were swaying gently from side to side. As the kittens leaped towards them they opened their mouths to try and gobble the ice cream of their choice. Or they could clutch one of the complete cones between their paws. The results were hilarious. Kittens fell to the floor, thoughtfully protected by thick foam mattresses, with blobs of ice cream all over their faces, their paws, and everywhere else you can think of.

The second enclosure was the **Scary I Scream Chamber.** This had blacked out sides so that none of the watching cats could see what was going on inside. When kittens entered the chamber they were immediately in a pitch black, damp and scary maze with slimy, slippery walls and floor. And on the walls were ghastly, scary things like wet seaweed and giant plastic creepy crawlies that felt horrible to the touch. Now you might think that all this would not present much of a problem to kittens, that they could just avoid the scary things, what with their being able to see in the dark. But that's where you'd be wrong. The architect-cat who had designed the chamber had used a specially manufactured paint that was impossible for cats to see. It was applied to all surfaces and all the freaky, scary items in the chamber. All those kittens who entered the chamber were unable to see anything at all, except a series of silver arrows painted on the floor to guide them to the exit. The chamber also had a fantastic sound system which relayed the frightened screams of the kittens to the loudspeakers on the outside of the chamber. Much to the amusement of the parent-cats relaxing outside the chamber. When the kittens came out of the chamber they were given a quick shower, followed immediately by a fabulous ice cream.

The walls of the Kitty Kat Ice-Cream Parlour were plastered with advertising slogans, all designed to whet the appetite of the customer-cats.

****

Have a really cool day – eat an ice-cream!

Treat yourself to a glorious Knickerbocker Glory!

Try our Banana Surprise – it's sure to surprise you!

Low fat Frozen Yoghurts – The healthy option!

*Take home our fantastic ice cream toothpaste -
Makes brushing your teeth a pleasure!*

When Stanley Smartpants and Derek Dimwit walked into the Kitty Kat Ice Cream Parlour, a wave of nostalgia swept over Stanley. "Gosh, Chief," he said, "this brings back squintillions of memories. I used to pester my mother constantly to bring me here when I was a kitten. It was soooo cool to be here."

"You're lucky, Stan," said Derek sadly. "We never had anything like this where I was brought up."

"Where was that, Chief?"

"Huh! You'll laugh, Stan."

"No I won't. You know I'm a sensitive cat."

"I was brought up in a broken down, abandoned shed on a bombed out piece of waste ground backing onto a railway line. In a dingy part of East London."

Stanley attempted a sympathetic, understanding smile. But it came across as more of a grimace.

"I know," said Derek, thinking it a grimace.

A young female cat came towards them. She was a gorgeous Ragamuffin with blue eyes, a white blaze in the centre of her sweet face, and a blue-grey bushy tail. She was wearing an incredible cotton dress, printed with pictures of ice cream cones, fruit sundaes, banana splits and knickerbocker glories.

"Wow!" said Stanley.

She smiled a wide, welcoming smile. "I guess you must be the cat-police. You're a bit different from our usual customers."

"Is it that obvious? Well, I'm Detective Sergeant Smartpants, and this is Detective Chief Inspector Dimwit."

"I've been expecting you. I'm Lollilop Lola, the manageress-cat." She put out her paw. Noticing the curious look on Derek's face she added, "we give away a free lollipop to all customer-kittens, so they all call me Lollilop Lola. Come, we'll sit at a table away from the hustle and bustle. Can I get you both an ice cream?"

"I was hoping you'd ask," said Stanley without a moment's hesitation.

"What about you, Chief Inspector?"

"Thank you, that would be nice. What do you recommend?"

"You could have a ***Banana Surprise.***"

"What's the surprise?" asked Derek.

Lola laughed. It was more of a cackle than a laugh, and it sounded like the laugh of a wicked witch.

"Ah well, you see, it's got everything you can think of in it. The fruits and the ice creams are heaped on top of each other in a long, tall black glass, so you can't see what's underneath each layer. Everyone is waiting for the banana, wondering if it's in the next layer. And then you get the surprise. There isn't any banana!" Lola laughed again, and her whole body shook with pleasure.

"I seem to remember that from when I was a kitten," said Stanley. "My mother used to bring me here. On one of our visits, when I was quite young, I wrote my very first poem.

When you're sitting round the pool,
Eating ice cream's oh so cool!"

"Look over there," said Lola, pointing at the nearest wall with her paw. "That's our house poem – it's been there for years. Perhaps you remember seeing it?"

Stanley read it out:

"Ice cream, nice cream,
We all scream for ice cream.
Ice cream a penny a lump,
The more you eat the more you jump!

Of course I remember it. That's what got me started writing poems. Mind you it's a long time since you could get an ice cream for a cat-penny."

"I'll tell you what you should have. Our **Red Fruits Extravaganza**. It's our most popular sundae in the summer."

"I'm almost afraid to ask what's in it."

"Let it be a surprise for you, Sergeant. I *can* give you one clue. It'll complement your outfit!" Lola laughed again. Stanley was wearing bright red trousers, a vivid plum waistcoat and a dark red bow tie.

Lola showed the two cat-police officers to a table in one corner of the store, where they would be able to talk freely without being overheard. She beckoned to one of the waitress-cats who came over to their table. She was a White Cornish Rex with large pointed ears that were seriously pink. She too was wearing the brightly coloured cotton dress with prints of fruits and ice cream sundaes.

"What would you like?" she asked.

"They're both going to have a Red Fruits Extravaganza," said Lola.

"A very good choice if I may say so." The waitress-cat stared pointedly at Stanley's waistcoat and trousers. She smiled at her own humour as she walked away.

"Let's get down to cat-business, Lola," said Stanley. "Tell us what happened."

"As you know the robbery took place some time yesterday. Or more accurately it was discovered yesterday afternoon."

"About what time?"

"About three o'clock."

"Who made the discovery?"

"I did."

"What exactly was stolen, Lola?"

"About five to six hundred cat-euros."

"Where was it stolen from?"

"The petty cash tin."

"Surely you don't keep your money in a petty cash tin?" said Derek.

"Of course not. We have a wall safe in the basement. Usually the petty cash has only a few cat-euros in it, but I didn't transfer all of the day's takings into the safe on Tuesday evening, because I knew that the painter-cat was coming to collect some cash. We've been having some decorating done. It was when he came to collect his money that I discovered the theft."

"Where do you keep the petty cash tin?" asked Stanley.

"In my office desk."

"Was the desk locked?"

"Yes. The thief-cat had forced the desk drawer. As a matter of fact he'd forced open four of the drawers."

"What about the petty cash tin itself. Was it locked? Was it broken into?"

"Yes it was locked, not that that mattered. The thief-cat took the whole tin."

"Hmm." Stanley thought for a few moments. "We'll need a complete list of your staff. It would also be helpful if you could give us a list of other cats who come here regularly."

"Gosh, Sergeant, that would be impossibly difficult. We have so many customers."

"I wasn't thinking of customer-cats. I mean cleaners, delivery drivers, tradescats, window cleaner-cat. That sort of thing. Any cats you accept without question. Any cats, apart from your staff, who might know where you keep money on the premises. Any cats whom you know have seen you go to the petty cash tin in your office desk."

"Of course, Sergeant. I'll organise it for later today."

"Have you noticed anything out of the ordinary, anything suspicious, over the last couple of days?"

"Nothing I can think of."

The waitress-cat was approaching their table, carrying a silver tray. The **Red Fruits Extravaganza** was presented in a large glass bowl. It was piled high with strawberries, raspberries, redcurrants and cherries. The four fruits were accompanied by four different ice creams. There was a raspberry sorbet, cream of Cornish vanilla, pistachio, and finally frozen pineapple yoghurt. As if all that wasn't enough, the luscious fruits and delicious ice creams were topped with lashings of real Devon clotted cream.

"Awesome!" exclaimed Stanley, as the bowl was put in front of him. He couldn't wait to tuck in, and picked up his spoon hungrily. "This is soooo cool!"

"Yes, it's a real treat," said Derek. "I think we can

put robbery talk on hold for the moment, don't you Stan?" He too couldn't wait to put a spoonful into his mouth.

The moment lasted twenty-five minutes. They ate alternately fast and slow. Fast when they just couldn't wait to get another mouthful, and slow when they wanted to make the delicious sensations last for ever. It took them the best part of fifteen minutes to finish the extravaganza, and almost as long to enjoy the inescapable ritual of licking their chops and cleaning their fur. The whole time they were eating and preening, Lola spent sitting contentedly looking on, her face full of happiness, her chest puffed out with pride. She simply loved it when her customer-cats were so obviously enjoying themselves.

"I can tell you one thing, Lola," said Stanley, still cleaning his head with his paw. "Without doubt that was better than a slap in the eye with a wet fish!"

Lola laughed, gazed at Stanley with admiration, and fluttered her eyelashes. Stanley appeared not to notice. "I did think of something while you were eating," she said. "One of the waitress-cats did notice a cat hanging around a few days ago, pacing up and down on the pavement, as if he was hungry."

Derek looked meaningfully at Stanley, but said nothing.

"Can we have a word with her?" said Stanley.

"She's not in today."

"Pity. Did she tell you anything about the cat? Any description?

"He was a male cat, but she didn't know what breed he was. He was shorthaired, blue with a silvery sheen."

"Did she mention any distinguishing features?"

"Not that I can think of."

"Did she mention whether or not he had a limp?"

"Did he have a limp?" she repeated, thinking hard. "No," she said finally, "she didn't mention anything about a limp."

"When is the waitress-cat next on duty?"

"Tomorrow morning."

"Just one more question. Did you find a dead mackerel in your desk?"

"Good gracious no! Should I have done? Oh, I understand. The mackerel robberies that were mentioned in the Cat-Haven Chronicle. Do you think this robbery was connected with them?"

"It's a bit early to say. We do need to examine the scene, Lola. Can you take us there?"

"Of course," said Lola pleasantly, and she got up from her chair.

They examined Lola's desk first of all. The fact that it had been broken into indicated that the thief-cat expected to find something. That four of the six drawers had been forced led Stanley to conclude that the thief-cat didn't know in which drawer the petty cash tin would be found. There were no obvious clues in or around the desk. Under the desk there was a waste paper basket. Stanley examined it. "Huh! Would I be right in thinking that you didn't have your office cleaned last night, Lola?"

Lola looked surprised. "Yes, that's right. It was the cleaner's night off. How did you know?"

"Your waste paper basket obviously wasn't emptied last night. If it had been, you'd have been told about it."

"About what?"

Stanley smiled a thin smile, without humour. "There's a skeleton of a mackerel in it!"

"Goodness me! I guess that means our robbery *is* connected with the others."

"I would say so, Lola."

They searched every inch of Lola's office, and were just about to give up when Stanley found a single blue hair on the back of Lola's desk chair. He gave it to Derek to put into a plastic bag. "I'd like to send in our forensic cats later this afternoon. Just in case they can come up with something."

"No problem."

"I guess that about wraps it up for now. Let me have your phone number in case there's anything else I want to ask you." Stanley took out his work mobile and entered Lola's number. "And perhaps *you* can ring me when you've got your list together? I'll send one of our cats down to collect it. You never know, I might even come down and collect it myself. Particularly if you invite me to sample another of your delicious ice creams." Stanley gave Lola an enormous wink.

"Of course, Sergeant, it would be my pleasure."

"Oh, call me Stan, everyone else does."

"Well, Stan, you can come here for an ice cream anytime!"

Derek felt slightly hurt that Lola hadn't invited him as well.

20

Friday 14th July

It was lunchtime at the Cat-Police Station. Yesterday Greta the Grumbler had cooked a chicken dish, and it had gone down well with most of the cats. Unfortunately she'd cooked much too much and there was plenty left over. She knew that Chief Inspector Dimwit was a stickler when it came to wastage. He simply hated it, and demanded that Greta re-heat any left over food. Today she had done exactly that. The dining room was full, and the cats of the Cat-Haven Cat-Police were ready and waiting for their lunch, their mouths watering already. When Greta brought in the huge bowls of yesterday's chicken there were groans and miaows galore round the table.

"Not chicken again, surely?" complained Pamela.

"Wait a minute," said Marmaduke, "that looks like the same casserole Greta gave us yesterday. She's havin' a laugh. It's just not good enough. I'd rather have toast and marmalade."

"I'd rather have boiled eggs and soldiers," said Cynthia.

Studious Stephen looked up from his book, and took just a quick glance at the chicken casserole. "When I was at cat-police school we never had the same meal two days running." He returned to his book.

"Oh dear!" said Vinnie, "I don't think I'll be able to eat it anyway. I think I need to go for a poo. In a hurry." He got up from the table and shot towards the door like a scorched rabbit.

Three of the newer cadet-cats took one look at what was on offer, got up from the table, and just walked away.

Tammy was a real fussy diva. She always took a slow, uninterested, sniffy look at every meal that was put in front of her. Several scornful sniffs and a few moments of thought later, she would toss her head, and swish her tail dramatically. Then with a great show of contempt she would walk slowly away, her nose in the air. Of course, mostly she would return a few minutes later and sit down to eat. As was her custom, she went through her comical charade now. She sniffed the chicken stew three times. Sniff, sniff, sniff, she sniffed! And then without saying a word she stalked off.

"I bet she won't come back to the table today," said

Jack. "It's simply not Tammy's style to eat yesterday's leftovers. All the more for me. Yum, yum!" He grinned and spooned a large portion of chicken into his bowl. He licked his whiskers hungrily.

Derek Dimwit was also disappointed, particularly since he was starving. He had to force himself to eat it. But eat it he did. As a matter of principle.

Despite all the complaints and catty remarks about Greta's cooking, most of the cat-police ate a hearty enough lunch. Stanley, who was also the cat-wine steward, had chosen a delicately perfumed white wine from the South of France to accompany today's lunch. Cadet-cats, of course, were only allowed to have soft drinks, but all cats from the rank of cat-constable upwards were able to enjoy a single glass of wine with their lunch.

A short catnap after lunch was perfectly acceptable in the Cat-Haven cat-police force, and most cats went to the rest and play room. There was a dart board and a pool table, a tea and coffee machine, and loads of comfy armchairs. There were four computer screens, one for internal cat-police business, two for playing games, and one with a permanent connection to the internet. There were two televisions, at opposite ends of the room, one of which was permanently tuned to Sky-Cat News. The other one was tuned to one of the Sky-Cat Sports channels. Today it was showing the Cat-Tour de France, the greatest cat-cycling race in the world. Scattered around were several copies of the Cat-Haven Chronicle, and a few of the Cat-Police Gazette. It was fair to say that the police-cats of Cat-Haven led a very pampered existence, as indeed was their expectation.

Studious Stephen continued reading his book, a history of the Egyptian Cat-Pyramids. Jack and Marmaduke played a game of pool, a couple of the young cadet-cats played Simpsons Hit and Run on the Playstation, and almost all the other cats had a snooze.

After lunch Stanley had gone back to his office to catch up on his paperwork. He pulled out his mobile phone and dialled Lola's number. The call went straight through to her voicemail. He decided not to leave a message, but send her a text instead.

"Hi Lola. Trying 2 contact u"

Lola's response was almost immediate. *"Hi stan how r u?"*

Stan replied. *"Gr8 how r u? Did u speak 2 ur waitress?"*

"Just now. Cat didnt limp. Do u want 2 no anything else?"

"No thanx. C u later"

Stanley flipped the lid of his mobile closed. He had called a meeting of all the cat-constables and cadet-cats in the Crime Room for three o'clock. He checked his watch – it was five to three. He got up from his swivel chair, straightened his cream and mid-brown check trousers and tucked in his plain, dark brown short sleeved cotton shirt. He crossed the corridor to the Crime Room.

His cats drifted in for the meeting in dribs and drabs. Stanley could tell from their eyes that some of them were still half asleep. It concerned him that they might be less than sharp and attentive. However, once they were all assembled he opened the meeting just before half past three.

"OK, cats," he said, "we're here to have a thorough review of the Mackerel Robberies case. Marmaduke has done a splendid job producing the Incident Board that you all see in front of you." Many of the younger cat-cadets turned towards Marmaduke, who made a great play of taking out his marmalade coloured handkerchief and blowing his nose.

"I want you all to study it before we open the discussion," said Stanley.

Cat-Haven Cat-Police
CASE: Mackerel Robberies
CRIME SCENES

INCIDENT BOARD

Last updated: Last updated: 13th July 2008

DATE	LOCATION	CRIME	CLUES	OTHER INFO
Thurs 6 July	Granny Garbo's House	Robbery — cash stolen from top of wardrobe in Granny's bedroom	Pawprint on dressing table 2 blue hairs found	
Friday 7 July	Cat Diamonds "R" Us	Cash stolen from till Diamond necklace stolen from shop window	Blue hair found, and piece of grey cotton — torn from grey jeans (made in China)	Cat seen hanging around, silvery blue coat, shabbily dressed, had a limp.
Sat 8 July	Skating Rink	Cash stolen from till	Blue hair found	Cat seen hanging around, probably blue-grey, had a limp
Mon 10 July	Cat-Odeon	Safe broken into	Pawprint on safe	
Wed 12 July	Kitty Kat Ice-Cream Parlour	Petty Cash tin stolen from desk	Blue hair found	Cat seen hanging around, blue

Cat-Haven Cat-Police
CASE: Mackerel Robberies
SUSPECTS & OTHERS

INCIDENT BOARD

Last updated: 13ᵗʰ July 2008

SUSPECTS	COLOUR/BREED	INFORMATION TO HAND
Beastly Boris aka Yuri Katakov	Russian Blue	Dishwasher at Cluck Cluck – ? illegal immigrant? Flew to Malaga Tues 11th July
Klepto Klaws	Sphynx — black, hairless	Known to be a fence but has never been prosecuted
Sing Song	Blue Burmilla	Admitted buying stolen necklace
Vladimir Katakov	Russian Blue	? brother of Yuri — Handycat at the Cat-Odeon. ? also illegal immigrant
Mystery Cat	Blue-grey or silver blue Breed not known	Seen at — Cat Diamonds "R" Us, Skating Rink, Kitty Kat Ice Cream Parlour
Larry Cluck Cluck	Norwegian Forest Cat Brown/black	Employs illegal immigrants – almost for sure

168

Cat-Haven Cat-Police
CASE: Mackerel Robberies
COMPUTER INFO

INCIDENT BOARD

Last updated: 13ᵗʰ July 2008

SUSPECTS	COLOUR/BREED	INFORMATION TO HAND
Albert Tartpincher	Blue Burmese	Window Cleaner-cat at Cat-Diamonds "R" Us, Skating Rink, Cat-Odeon. Arrested over theft of pineapple tarts 6 months ago.
Spit and Polish	Blue Burmese	Hungarian cleaner-cat at Skating Rink, Cat-Odeon, Kitty Kat Ice Cream Parlour
Cauliflower Colin	Blue Korat	Projectionist-cat at Cat-Odeon
Billy Blunderhead	Blue Korat	Waiter-cat at Cluck Cluck Diner
Saucy Suzette	Blue Ocicat	French Chef at Chez Les Chats
Calculating Calvin	Russian Blue	Bookkeeper-cat at Kitty Kat Ice Cream
Ten Bangles Tonia	Russian Blue	Sales-cat at Cat-Diamonds "R" Us

"Right, let's see if we can eliminate any of the suspects," said Stanley. "I think we can discount Sing Song. Since we're pretty certain that he paid Klepto Klaws for the necklace, that alone would indicate that he isn't the thief. Any comments?" he asked, looking round the table.

"Even a blind cat with a wooden leg would realise that," said Chief Inspector Dimwit. No other cat had anything to say.

"All right, let's remove Sing Song. What about Klepto Klaws? Who'd like to start with him?"

"The fact that he's not a blue cat rules him out doesn't it?" said Studious Stephen.

"You're havin' a laugh," said Marmaduke. "You can't rule anybody out at this early stage. Although he might not be the cat who's actually stealing the cat-euro cash, perhaps he's the mastermind? Perhaps he's organising other cats to do it?"

"You could put Larry Cluck Cluck in the same category," said Tammy. "From everything I've heard said, he's a pretty unsavoury character, a grasping businesscat. Isn't he employing illegal immigrants? Perhaps he's using some of *them* to pull off all the robberies?"

"Both ideas are interesting, but I don't think they help us too much," said Stanley. "We know we'll never get an admission like that out of Klepto Klaws, and no doubt the same would apply to Larry Cluck Cluck. We've found blue hairs at four of the five crime scenes, which is a pretty clear indication that the thief-cat is blue. Regardless of any involvement Klepto Klaws or Larry Cluck Cluck might have, we must concentrate on the fact that it's a blue cat who is committing the crimes."

"I still think it's Beastly Boris," said Derek Dimwit.

"It's hardly likely," said Stephen scornfully. "The fact of the matter is, we know he left the country the day before the robbery at the Kitty Kat Ice Cream Parlour." Several of the cadet-cats laughed. Stephen licked his fur in an exaggerated manner, and adjusted his glasses on the bridge of his nose.

Jumping Jack opened his mouth in a massive yawn, showing all his teeth. "Miaow-ow-ow-ow," he yawned. More laughter.

"Excuse me Sergeant Smartpants," said Soppy Cynthia hesitantly, "but what does aka mean?"

"It's a cat-police term, Cynthia," said Stanley. "It stands for also known as."

"Sorry about this Sarge," said Vinnie, looking really uncomfortable. "I need to go for a poo" Even more laughter, as Vinnie bunny-hopped out of the Crime Room.

Jack yawned again in the same exaggerated manner. "Miaow-ow-ow-ow." He looked around hoping to get a reaction from the other cats. He got it! There was lots more laughter, and he looked ever so pleased with himself.

"You are awful, Jack," said Cynthia, a look of delight on her face.

"What do you call a cat with a banana stuffed in both ears, Cyn?" said Jack, winking at Cynthia.

"Dunno, Jack."

"Anything you like, Cyn! Ha! Ha! Ha!"

Cynthia clapped her paws in delight.

"I don't get that," said Studious Stephen with a frown.

Once more Jack yawned a massive yawn, drawing laughs from most of the cats in the room. "You are pretty dumb sometimes, Stephen. You can call him whatever names you like 'cos with a banana in each ear he can't hear anything."

Stanley loved it when his cats were having fun, but realised that the situation was gradually getting out of hand, and he knew that he had to regain control. "You think that's clever do you, Jack?" The smirk on Jack's face suggested that he did. "Let me tell you this, Jack ......

> *To yawn a lot makes you look bored.*
> *Of this you can but be assured,*
> *Not only is it really rude,*
> *You'll never be the coolest dude!"*

Gales of laughter swept round the crime room. Every cat knew that Jack liked to think of himself as a 'cool dude'. And he flushed with embarrassment.

"Let's return to Beastly Boris," said Stanley. "The truth of the matter is that we don't know for a fact that Boris *has* left the country. We only have one cat's word for it. Marmaduke, you took the call about Boris, didn't you? Can you look up your notes and give us a bit more information."

Sitting out of Stanley's vision so that he could eat without being seen, Marmaduke had just stuffed a piece of toast and marmalade into his mouth. Stanley's question made him jump with surprise. As a result, the piece of toast got stuck in his windpipe, and he began to wheeze and gasp for breath. Jack summed up the situation immediately and rushed over to his friend. Only last week in their first aid class they had all been taught the Heimlich-cat manoeuvre, more commonly known as the catsgullet technique. He stood behind Marmaduke, whose face was already turning blue, and locked his paws together round Marmaduke's chest. He then performed several sharp, upward thrusts with his paws. Much to everyone's relief the piece of toast became dislodged, and it flew out of Marmaduke's mouth. It shot across the room like an arrow and struck Chief Inspector Dimwit smack in the face. By now it wasn't so much a piece of toast, but more a soggy ball of mulched bread covered in marmalade and saliva.

"Yuck!" exclaimed Tammy.

Jack just about managed to hold himself in check, when what he really wanted was to laugh out loud.

"Sorry, Chief," said Marmaduke. "Couldn't be helped."

Pamela rubbed Marmaduke's back. "Are you all right, Marmy," she said, concern etched on her face.

"Do you feel ok to continue, Marmy?" said Stanley sympathetically.

"Yes, Sarge. I'm fine." Marmaduke pulled out his notebook. "Now when exactly was it?" he said, more to himself than anyone else. "It was Tuesday, wasn't it? Two days ago." As usual Marmaduke made a great drama of flipping over the pages of his notebook, and studying every page carefully. "Yes," he said at last, "here it is. Mmmm, it doesn't tell us much. Just that a member of the cat-public rang in and said, and I quote his actual words .... I've just seen Beastly Boris go through the boarding gate to catch a flight to Malaga ..... and then *I* said .... how do you know it was Beastly Boris? And then *he* said .... I recognised him from his photograph in yesterday's edition of the Cat-Haven Chronicle. And then *I* said .... I see .... and then *he* said .... I'm quite sure it was him. And then *I* said ....

Stanley shook his head in frustration, but bit his tongue.

.... can you give me your name and address, sir. And then the line went dead. That was it." Marmaduke snapped his notebook closed.

"Do you remember anything else about the call, Marmaduke?"

"I did think at the time that he spoke cat-lingo with a bit of a foreign accent. "Like Eastern European or something."

"Is it possible, Sarge," said Jack trying to get back into Stanley's good books, "that it was Beastly Boris himself who made the phone call?"

"That's a clever observation, Jack. It's not like we've had squintillions of calls, is it? In fact not one other cat has rung in with the same story. I think we have to assume that he *is* still in the country. And that means that he is still our prime suspect."

"As I've said all along," said Derek, "it *must* be Beastly Boris. Everything points to it."

"Boris might well be the criminal-cat, Chief," said Stephen, "but we have to keep an open mind. That's what they taught us in cat-police school."

"I realise that," said Derek Dimwit sharply, "I'm not completely stupid. I was just expressing an opinion, that's all."

Stanley jumped in, aware that once again the Chief had made a fool of himself in front of his detective-cats. "Let's consider Vladimir Katakov. It's a fair bet that he and Beastly Boris, whose real name is Yuri Katakov remember, are related. Have we made any progress, Jack, on establishing where he lives?"

"Me and Marmaduke went to the Cat-Odeon yesterday, and managed to get the staff roster. He was off yesterday and is off today, but he's back at work on Monday."

"What time does he finish?"

"Five thirty."

"Right, I want you and Marmaduke to follow him when he leaves the Cat-Odeon." Stanley paused to pick up the internal telephone. "Greta," he said, "did you book Francesca's flight to California? …… When is she going? ….. Thanks." Stanley put the phone down. "Francesca's travelling to California later today so that she can use the Catmel forensic equipment to work on the breed of the criminal-cat. Hopefully we'll have some news from her by the early part of next week. Once we know the breed it will narrow down our search."

"Who is Albert Tartpincher, Stan?" asked Derek Dimwit. "The name sounds familiar."

"It should do, Chief. You arrested him six months ago."

"*I* did?"

"You suspected him of stealing pineapple tarts from the Cat-Haven cat-bakery, don't you remember?"

Marmaduke interrupted. "I remember that, Chief. You said that with a name like Tartpincher it was a racing certainty that he was, and I remember your words exactly, 'the cat wot dunnit'." A few laughs and several giggles went round the table. "Mind you, with your record of losing bets on the horses, there's no such thing as a racing certainty!"

Chief Inspector Dimwit pretended that he had no recollection of the incident. But Marmaduke wasn't about to let his boss off the hook so easily. "You *must* remember. I was with you at the time. We were investigating a series of thefts of pineapple tarts. And when you saw him running out of the cat-bakery with a big bagful of pineapple tarts, you nabbed him by the collar. You asked him his name, and as soon as he said Albert Tartpincher you arrested him. We took him straight back to the station. You didn't stop to ask the assistant-cat in the cat-bakery if Albert had paid for the tarts. It turned out that he *had* paid for them, and he was running for a bus! He threatened to sue the Cat-Haven Cat-Police, and you personally, for wrongful arrest. It was only Sergeant Smartpants' intervention that saved the day. You *must* remember all this, Chief!"

"That's enough, Marmaduke," said Stanley.

At that moment Vincent returned to the Meeting Room looking much happier.

"I know a joke about a cat-bakery," said Jack.

"Another time, Jack," said Stanley.

"Why is he called Albert Tartpincher, Sarge, if he didn't steal the pineapple tarts?" said Pamela.

"He was accused of stealing squintillions of jam tarts from the Albert Hall. But there was no proof. He denied it, of course. Said he'd never been anywhere near the Albert Hall, had never even been to London. But he kind of got stuck with the name."

"He's certainly not the mysterious blue cat that's been seen at three of the crime scenes," said Stephen.

"What makes you say that?" asked Stanley.

"Since he cleans their windows, they would have recognised him, wouldn't they?" said Stephen smugly.

"I wouldn't have thought of that," said Derek Dimwit. "But he could still be the thief-cat. Maybe he had another cat checking out the crime scenes for him?"

"He wouldn't need to, would he?" said Stephen. "The fact of the matter is he's probably there once a week cleaning the windows!"

"I hear what you say, Stephen, but it doesn't change the fact that he's still the p-p-p-p-p-p-prime suspect."

Stanley coughed. "Ahem. The most interesting feature of the case to me is the appearance of the blue-coloured cat a day or two before the robberies. One witness thinks he was blue-grey, and the other two think he was silvery blue. I don't have any doubts that it's the same cat. It seems pretty unlikely that there would be two different cats checking out the crime scenes. I feel very strongly that this blue cat is involved in the crimes. Either he *is* the criminal-cat or he's working for the actual thief. Either way, I think that if we can find him, we'll solve the case."

"Are you sure there aren't two cats, Stan?" said Derek. "The witnesses at Cat Diamonds and at the Cluck Cluck said that the blue cat had a limp. But the cat seen at the Skating Rink didn't."

"I can't explain that, Chief, but I suspect there is

only one cat. As for the other cats that the computer has thrown up, we need to interview all of them, and I'll work out who does what a bit later. The one that seems to be of the most interest is the Hungarian cleaner-cat, Spit and Polish. Jack, I'd like you and Marmaduke to question him as soon as you can."

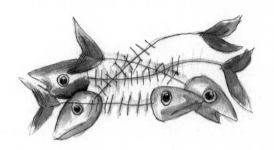

Saturday 15th July

S tanley Smartpants was hoping to have a day
off. But no such luck! He got a call on his office
mobile phone from Cheerful Charlie. There'd
been another robbery.

Stanley was a seriously cool cat, and he had two
mobile phones. One was his office mobile, which he
used for cat-police business only, and the other was his
personal mobile. He'd had three texts on his personal
mobile that morning. There was one from Peaches, one
from Lola and one from Katie. Often he would prepare
drafts of texts he would send later. But there was an
obvious danger in this, which Stanley was well aware
of. He would have to be extra careful to ensure that he
sent the right text to the right cat! He was just smiling
to himself at this thought when his office mobile rang.

****

The robbery had occurred at the Feline Furniture Emporium, a furniture megastore in the Retail Park on the edge of town. Stanley had already dressed in one of his favourite summer weekend outfits. He wore a pair of close fitting white Burberry jeans, with a black leather belt, and a blue and white diamond check tank top. He decided not to change into something more formal, and rang Derek Dimwit, who was spending a quiet Saturday morning at home. With great reluctance Derek agreed to go with Stanley to the furniture store.

It really was a *mega* store carrying a complete range of domestic furniture. They had the largest selection of beds and mattresses in the whole of Cat-Haven. But their speciality was the vast range of comfy chairs and sofas, all of them designed for a cat to have a short and luxuriously comfortable catnap. The owner was a second generation British muslim-cat, his grandparents having come to Britain from Pakistan many years ago. He was an Asian Chocolate Smoke with pale green eyes, and generally regarded as very handsome. He was known as Mr Forty Winks. He greeted Stanley and Derek with a frown on his handsome brown face.

"Oh dear," he said, "I knew I should have gone to the bank yesterday. I was too involved in watching the Cat-Open golf on television. I've had a bet on Tiger-Cat Forrest to win it, you know. Oh dear, my wife has always said that golf would be my downfall. It seems that she's been right all along." He wrung his paws in an exaggerated gesture of despair.

"What actually happened, Mr Winks?" asked Stanley.

"I came in to open the shop this morning as usual, and found that the safe had been forced open with an iron bar of some sort. It's not a very good safe. In fact I bought it cheap at a car boot sale. I knew it wasn't a good investment. Oh dear! My wife told me at the time. She was right all along."

"How much was stolen, Mr Winks?"

"Approximately five thousand six hundred and twenty seven cat-euros, plus yesterday's takings. I didn't add them up yet. All in cash. I was too busy watching Tiger-Cat. My wife told me I should always make sure to add up the takings at the end of every day. So that I would always know how much money I had. Oh dear! She was right all along."

"We'd like to see where the safe is, Mr Winks."

Forty Winks took them into the back office. It was very cluttered, with paperwork all over the place. "Sorry about the mess," he said. "My wife's always telling me I should sort it out."

Stanley waited for the 'she was right all along' line, but on this occasion it didn't come. One look at the safe was enough to confirm Forty Winks' statement that the safe had been broken open with an iron bar. It was in a terrible state, the door virtually off its hinges. Stanley looked inside. It was completely empty except for one thing. "Look at this, Chief," he said. He picked up the skeleton of a dead mackerel. No particular surprise in that. But what did surprise both of the cat-police officers was the fact that the mackerel bones had been painted red.

Derek Dimwit had a puzzled look on his face "What does it mean, Stan?"

"I think he's trying to send us a message, Chief. Let's talk about it later. We have to bag this up and take it with us. Let's see if we can find anything else." It was not easy to search the office, it was in such a mess. They did their best but came up with nothing.

"What else can you tell us Mr Winks?"

Forty Winks suddenly decided to sharpen his claws on the carpet, and scratched away vigorously. Stanley and Derek looked on patiently, waiting for him to finish.

"Nothing," he said eventually. "I haven't seen anything suspicious. My wife always says I'm hopelessly unobservant. She's probably right. I can't see what's right in front of my nose, that's my trouble."

Forty Winks walked away from Stanley and Derek, towards one corner of the showroom. There was a huge scratching post which had been installed for the benefit of all the staff-cats. Forty Winks had had a lot of trouble in the early days of the business with many of his staff-cats using the brand new furniture for sharpening their claws! He went up to the scratching post, arched his back and stretched out his front paws.

He began scratching furiously.

"This is a real nuisance, Stan," grumbled Derek. "I'm going to the big football match between the Cat-Haven Gooners and Livercat. I'll be late if he doesn't get a move on.

Stanley smiled.

> "Be patient, Chief, and just you wait,
> I tell you true you won't be late.
> It won't take long for him to scratch.
> For sure you will not miss the match!"

"I hear what you say, Stan, but it doesn't help."

It was in fact only a few minutes before Forty Winks came back to join them.

"Have you seen a stranger-cat hanging around?" Stanley asked.

"No, sorry."

"Do you employ a cleaner-cat?"

"Yes, I do. He comes once a week. He's called Spit and Polish."

Stanley noted this fact with interest, but showed no outward sign that it meant anything to him. Derek Dimwit was about to say something, but one look at Stanley's face told him that it would be unwise.

"We'll send the forensic cats down later Mr Winks."

Forty Winks seemed to have shrunk in size. He was really upset. "My insurance only covers me for five hundred cat-euros in cash. My wife told me it wasn't enough. But I didn't want to pay the extra money the insurance company wanted. Insurance is so expensive, you know. And it's hard enough to make a decent living. Oh dear! She was right, of course. I'm not looking forward to telling her, you know. You'd think that she would be sympathetic, wouldn't you? But she won't be. You don't know her. She'll give me a right tongue-lashing. And she'll probably box my ears and pull my whiskers for good measure. Oh dear!"

Stanley felt really sorry for the furniture store owner-cat. "Come now, Mr Winks, this isn't doing you any good," he said sympathetically. "Try and be positive, look on the bright side."

"What bright side? There isn't one."

"Why don't you take a rest, Mr Winks," said Derek. "Sit down and have a rest in one of your own comfy chairs, and have a snooze."

"You mean have forty winks, don't you? Very funny, I'm sure!"

"We'll send in the forensic cats on Monday," said Stanley, "to see if the thief has left any clues for us, anything for our forensic department to work on."

"Won't it be a bit late by then? Why can't they come in today, while the trail is still hot?"

"I'm sorry, Mr Winks, but the forensic cats don't work at weekends."

"That's a bit unprofessional isn't it?"

"I don't want to bore you with the politics of it, Mr

Winks, but it's a question of resources. Our budget just won't stretch to having a 24/7 forensic department. There just isn't enough money in the kitty."

"I bet they've got enough money in the kitty at the Kitty Kat Ice Cream Parlour!" said Derek.

"I take it you specialise in funny remarks that aren't very funny," said Forty Winks, glaring at Derek.

"That wasn't very tactful, Chief," said Stanley once they were out of earshot.

"I hear what you say, Stan, but I didn't mean the snooze thing to come out like that. It wasn't *meant* to be a joke. I admit the kitty business *was*, but it wasn't said *against* him."

"That's as maybe, Derek, but when a cat's just been robbed, when he's lost a lot of cat-euro cash, he doesn't appreciate a slap in the eye with a wet fish. He doesn't really want to listen to jokes at his expense."

Derek Dimwit changed the subject. "You said that the thief-cat was trying to send us a message when he painted the dead mackerel red, Stan. What did you mean exactly?"

"You remember I said after the robbery at Cat Diamonds "R" Us that the mackerel business might be a red herring, to put us off, to send us in the wrong direction?"

"Yes."

"We've known for a long time that the mackerel

have got nothing to do with the actual crimes. Although they confirm that the same thief-cat is carrying out all the robberies."

"Why has he been leaving the skeleton of a mackerel at every crime scene?"

"That's a good question, Chief. Somehow, I don't think we'll know the answer to it until we catch him. Although I do have a theory."

"What is it?"

"I don't think he intended to leave the mackerel bones at Granny Garbo's. Remember, according to Francesca, the mackerel had been cooked in garlic butter, shallots and white wine. My guess is that he stole the mackerel simply to cook and eat them. He was eating one of them before he went in to Granny Garbo's house. Maybe he was still eating it when he entered the house. Maybe he didn't mean to leave it there. But once he *had* left it there, he thought it would be a good joke to leave one at Cat Diamonds "R" Us, and at the other crime scenes that came afterwards. This is the last mackerel, isn't it? He stole six mackerel, and this is the sixth robbery. Perhaps he painted it red as a final joke."

"Interesting theory, Stan. Now that the mackerel have run out, do you think this will be the last robbery?"

"It would be nice to think so, Chief. But I doubt it. In my experience these sorts of cats *never* stop. Not until they're caught. Anyway he can always get hold of more mackerel."

Monday 17th July

"There's a Harriet Fishnet here to see you, Sarge," said Greta the Grumbler, walking into Stanley Smartpants' office. "I hate to complain but I wish you'd get your intercom fixed so I don't have to walk up the stairs all the time. She says she was attacked as she was pulling her fishing boat out of the sea this morning." Greta ushered Harriet into Stanley's office. Stanley stood up to welcome her.

Harriet was an American Black Bombay with half of one front leg missing. Her smooth black coat gleamed in the sunshine that filtered through the office window, and her copper coloured eyes were bright and intelligent.

"Tell me what happened, Harriet," said Stanley.

"It must have been about seven o'clock this morning. Me and my brother had been out fishing for mackerel since about five o'clock. We pulled the boat up onto the sand on Torcat beach as usual. My brother went off to speak to one of his mates further up the beach. I started to offload the catch, ready to take it to the Fish Market, when I was struck from behind. I lost consciousness and when I came to I was lying on the ground beside my boat. Some of my mackerel catch was missing. I couldn't say how many fish were stolen, but probably a dozen or so."

"Did you see anything at all of your attacker?"

"No, nothing."

"Did you hear anything in the moments before the attack?"

"No."

"So you can't say whether you were attacked by a single cat or by more than one?"

"No."

"What about your brother? Did he see anything?"

"Unfortunately not. Sorry, I'm not being much help."

"Not at all, Harriet. It's good of you to come in. Is there anything at all you can add?"

"Not that I can think of."

"If anything occurs to you later, please give me a call." Stanley fished out a card from his waistcoat pocket and passed it to Harriet.

The early morning sun had disappeared, and the rain was lashing against the windows of the cat-police station. Stanley stepped out of his office and walked along the corridor. As he opened the door of the Crime Room a wall of noise hit him like a sledgehammer. Playful Pamela was chasing Jumping Jack round the room. Jack was leaping from one desk to another, with Pamela not far behind. The rest of the cat-constables and cadet-cats were screaming and shouting, cheering them on.

The moment Stanley stepped through the doorway, Jack came hurtling towards him. He was looking over his shoulder at the pursuing Pamela, and didn't see Stanley. He crashed into him, knocking him to the floor.

"Sorry, Sarge," he said breathlessly when he realised what had happened. Pamela came scudding towards them, and was unable to stop. Just as Stanley was trying to pick himself up, Pamela slammed into him, knocking him backwards.

"Oh sorry, Sarge," she blurted out. "I couldn't stop!"

The office fell silent, every cat waiting for Stanley's reaction. He clambered to his feet, and spoke softly.

> *It's good to jump and play and run,*
> *There's loads of time for lots of fun.*
> *But duty you must never shirk,*
> *'Cos when you're here you have to work.*

"Back to work everybody, please." The cat-constables and cadet-cats returned to their desks.

"We've just had a visit from Harriet Fishnet, the three-legged fishercat. A dozen or so mackerel were stolen from her this morning on Torcat beach. We don't know that this robbery is connected to our case, but my guess is that it *is*. I'd like you to add it to the Incident Board, Tammy. Right, let's have a progress report on some of the blue cats that we're interested in. Jack, I think you and Marmaduke have interviewed Spit and Polish, the Hungarian cleaner-cat, haven't you?" At that moment Chief Inspector Derek Dimwit came in to the office, carrying a cup of tea. "You're just in time, Chief, to hear about the Hungarian cleaner-cat."

Jack had calmed down now, although he was still sweating from his game with Pamela, and he wiped his brow with his paw. "Yes, Sarge. Me and Marmaduke caught up with him on Saturday afternoon. He lives in a tiny one-room bedsit near the harbour. It was so cramped with three of us in the room. There wasn't even room to swing a dog! He *is* a Blue Burmese, but he doesn't have a limp. His real name is Laszlo Kiss. Mind you, I wouldn't want to kiss him!" Jack looked round for some reaction from his companions. There were a few giggles. "I took a photo of him on my mobile phone. Here it is on the computer." Jack pulled up the picture on the large screen that hung next to the Incident Board.

"Oooh!" exclaimed Tammy. "I wouldn't mind kissing him. He's pretty lush!" Several other female cats miaowed their agreement. "I certainly fancy him," gushed Pamela. "He looks *very* kissable to me!"

Studious Stephen coughed. "Not many cats know this," he said, fingering his glasses, "but Kiss is the seventh most popular surname in Hungary."

"That's *really* interesting, Stephen," said Marmaduke rolling his eyeballs. The female cadet-cats laughed noisily and Stephen blushed.

"Let's get back to Laszlo Kiss," said Stanley.

"He was a bit difficult," continued Jack. "Didn't want to give us any information. He is legal though. He showed us his passport. I think he was just about to go out when we arrived, and he was anxious the whole time we were with him. He didn't want to tell us where he was going. He's been working as a cleaner-cat for six months now, but he wouldn't tell us how he got the work. Just that a friend had suggested the places to try. Basically he was on the defensive. After we left we hid round the corner and followed him. He went straight to the Magyar Palace, the Hungarian restaurant in town." Jack took out his notebook and flipped over the pages. "Yes," he said, "he arrived there at five past six. We didn't go in, but waited for the best part of an hour. He didn't come out, so we figured that he works there."

"Did you establish what his working hours are on his cleaning jobs?"

"Not really. It seems that he has a key to the premises in every case, and goes in some time overnight. No specific times. As long as he gets the offices clean, that's all that his employers are interested in."

"Well done, you two. Good cat-police work. Move his name up to the Suspects section please, Tammy. Perhaps I'll pay the Magyar Palace a visit, maybe even this evening. Now Stephen, tell us about your interview with Ten Bangles Tonia."

Studious Stephen put down his book on the Egyptian cat-pyramids, and opened his notebook. "Pamela and I visited Cat-Diamonds "R" Us on Saturday afternoon, at approximately three thirty seven, and spoke with Miss Ten Bangles Tonia. The fact of the matter is we can rule her out completely. She's just come back from a two week holiday in Florida. So she was out of the country when the robberies were committed. I've asked her to confirm the details of her holiday, for the record, and she said she would pop in to the station today with the paperwork."

Marmaduke spoke quietly to Jack. "The fact of the matter is," he said, mimicking Stephen's precise manner of speaking, "he's so terribly boring."

"Yeah," said Jack, "you can say that again. Hey, Marmy, I wonder if he bores himself as much as he bores other cats!"

Marmaduke couldn't help himself. He laughed like a mad cat.

Vacant Vincent raised his paw. There was a look of anxiety on his black face. "Sorry about this, Sarge, but I need to go for a poo. It's urgent." He jumped up out of his chair.

"Off you go, Vincent. Don't be long. Now, where were we?"

"I was just going to tell you," said Jack, "that me and Marmaduke are hoping to try and see the French chef at Chez Les Chats. If it stops raining, that is. Which reminds me ….." He jumped up onto his desk, so that he had the attention of every cat in the room. "Does anyone know why owls never mate when it's lashing down with rain?" No-one replied. "It's simple," he went on. "It's too wet to woo! Ha! Ha! Ha!"

Cynthia laughed the loudest of all the cats in the room. "Oh, you are awful, Jack," she said. She leaped to her feet, threw herself down on the floor and began to clutch at her ribs.

"What are you doing?" said Pamela.

"Jack's so funny, isn't he? I'm trying to tickle myself so I can carry on laughing."

"You can't tickle *yourself*," said Stephen scornfully. "That's a well known fact."

"Yes you can," said Marmaduke. "All you have to do is rub your ribs with the back of your claws. Anyone knows that."

"That's right," said Jack. "It's easy-peasy! Ha! Ha! Ha!"

"See, you don't know everything, clever clogs," said Marmaduke.

Stephen looked uncertain, and a little embarrassed.

Most of the cats in the room laughed. But not Tammy. Her face was a mask of gloom and doom.

"Sarge," she said softly, "everybody seems to have a job except me. Why haven't I got a job?"

After the incident in the air-conditioning warehouse, when Tammy had had a tantrum and threatened them with the industrial cat-tribunal, Stanley had resolved not to take her on any more outside jobs. But he didn't want her to know that, and approached the problem from a different angle.

"We need someone reliable to man the office and keep the Incident Board current. It's an important job, and I don't want to leave it to one of the cadet-cats. You're perfect for the job, Tammy. I know that I can rely on you."

"Of course you can, Sarge," said Tammy, feeling ten feet tall.

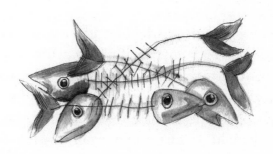

Monday 17th July

Later that morning, with the sun now shining out of a deep blue sky, Stanley Smartpants and Derek Dimwit walked into the office of Miserable Melvin at the Cat-Odeon.

"It's another miserable Monday," moaned Melvin, his voice overflowing with misery. "My cleaner-cat didn't turn up on Saturday night or last night. The place is a tip!"

Stanley wondered whether the visit of Jack and Marmaduke had anything to do with Spit and Polish not turning up. "I'm waiting for a couple of cats from the Catpower agency to turn up. We can't possibly open this afternoon with all this trash from Saturday night. I don't suppose you've got any news about the missing cash, have you?"

"Our investigation is proceeding well, Melvin," replied Derek, as if he was quoting from the rule book.

"I knew there was no point in asking," said Melvin with a miserably long face. "From what I've heard the Cat-Haven cat-police are clueless."

"That's a bit unfair," countered Stanley. "There are squintillions of crimes in Cat-Haven, and we solve most of them."

"But it's a week ago since the robbery, and I've heard nothing from you."

"Just because you haven't heard from us doesn't mean we're not working on the case, Melvin. Yours is one of six robberies that we're investigating. And we have already established that the crimes were committed by the same cat or cats. We're getting closer all the time. The reason we're here now is that we'd like to have a word with one of your projectionist-cats, Cauliflower Colin."

"Why is he called Cauliflower Colin?" asked Derek. "Is it because he's got cauliflower ears?"

"No," replied Melvin sharply. "If you must know it's because he eats cauliflower sandwiches while he's running the films."

"Cauliflower sandwiches!" said Derek in amazement. "That's a bit strange isn't it?"

"Perhaps we could see him," said Stanley, "with or without his cauliflower sandwich. Can you provide us with a room where we could talk to him?"

"You can use my office, Sergeant. I'll go and find him and ask him to come up." Miserable Melvin got up from his swivel chair and left the office.

"I wonder if he has cheese sauce with his cauliflower?" said Derek. "Mind, if he did, that would make it a bit gooey, wouldn't it? I've never heard of a cat eating cauliflower sandwiches. It's really odd."

"Give it a rest, Chief. We're here on serious cat-police business."

There was a knock at the door, and Cauliflower Colin entered the room. He was a Blue Korat with a short, silver-blue coat, a heart shaped face and large olive green eyes. Stanley noted that he did not limp.

"I believe you want to see me," he said without warmth.

"I'm Detective Sergeant Smartpants, and this is my colleague Detective Chief Inspector Dimwit," said Stanley formally. "Take a seat, please." He motioned with his paw to one of the office chairs, and took Melvin's swivel chair himself. "We understand, Colin, that there is a spare key to Melvin's office in the projection room."

"Yes, there is. It's hanging on a nail."

"Is the projection room locked at the end of the evening show?"

"Sometimes, but not always."

"Do you know if the door was locked last Sunday night, when the robbery took place?"

"I'll have to think about that." There was a long silence, interrupted only by the ticking of a clock on the office wall. Stanley examined his claws. I must have a manicure he said to himself. Eventually Cauliflower

Colin spoke again. "Truth is, I can't remember."

"Does the cleaner-cat have access to the projection room?"

"He only cleans it once a week. We always leave it unlocked when he's scheduled to clean it."

"When was the last time he cleaned it before the robbery?"

"Ah," exclaimed Colin, as if he'd had a sudden revelation. "He cleaned it the Sunday night of the robbery, so the door would have been unlocked."

"I see. Where were you at seven o'clock this morning, Colin?"

"At home in bed."

"Can anyone confirm that?"

"No, I live on my own."

"Is there anything *you'd* like to ask, Chief?"

Just for a moment Stanley thought that Derek might ask him if he had cheese sauce with his cauliflower sandwiches, but Derek simply shook his head.

Stanley got up from the swivel chair. "Thank you, Colin, that'll be all for now." He went round to the other side of the desk. "That's a really nice coat you have, Colin," he said running his paw over Colin's fur.

Colin swelled with pride. "Thank you," he said, "I brush it regularly." He didn't notice that as Stanley drew away his paw, he plucked a single blue hair from Colin's coat.

After Colin had left the office, Stanley deposited

the single blue hair in a plastic bag. "We'll take this for DNA analysis, and ask Francesca to compare it to the ones we found at the crime scenes."

"Sorry about this, Stan, but what exactly is DNA analysis again? I know you've explained it to me before, but I can't quite remember."

Stanley smiled, not at all upset that once again he had to explain basic cat-police procedure to his boss. "It's a bit complicated to explain DNA, chief. Put simply it's what makes us unique. Every cat in the world is unique, chief. There's no two cats the same. Let's consider this hair that we've taken from Colin. When it's analysed in the laboratory, that's to say examined in great detail, with the special equipment Francesca will bring back from California, it will tell us several different things ......"

"Like what breed the cat is," said Derek brightly, proud to show Stanley that he *did* remember *some* things.

"Exactly. That will be a great help to us because it will immediately eliminate most of the suspects. More important than that is the fact that we can discover whether two separate hairs come from the same cat, in other words are an *exact* match. No two cats in the world have the same DNA."

"I see ......" said Derek slowly, beginning to understand."

"We'll give her Colin's hair when she gets back, Chief. I wonder how she's getting on?"

24

Monday 17th July
Catmel-By-The-Sea, California

I n Cat-Haven-on-Sea, England, it was four o'clock in the afternoon of a warm summer's day. In the United States of America, in Catmel-by-the-Sea, California, it was eight o'clock in the morning of what would turn out to be a crushingly hot summer's day.

Apple Pie Annie stepped out of the coolness of her air-conditioned apartment, just ten small city blocks up from the ocean, into the already oven-like heat of the early morning. She was a striking, if slightly wild-looking, Blue California Spangled cat. Her long, lean body was marked with distinctive black stripes and spots, and she had stunning almond shaped olive green eyes that charmed every cat who looked into them. She had earned a Masters degree in forensic cat-medicine from Harvard-Cat University, and was employed as a forensic cat by the Catmel County Cat-

Police Department.

She strolled down the steep slope of Seafood Boulevard towards the sea, and stopped at the baker's shop to buy a couple of apple pies for her lunch. It was her favourite street in the whole of Catmel, and her favourite part of it was the block nearest the ocean which was jam-packed with swanky, fancy schmancy seafood restaurants. Only last night she had enjoyed oysters on the half shell at one of them, Oysters Unlimited. Cats never go hungry for seafood treats in Catmel!

She spotted her uncle on the other side of the street, unlocking the glass door of the art gallery he owned. Annie called out to attract his attention, and waved vigorously. She walked to work every morning, an experience of contrasting emotions. She loved the smell of the trees that were planted in the middle of the road, and the rustle of their leaves when there was a cooling breeze. But she hated the smell of the freshly deposited poops that pet dogs had left littering the sidewalks. At the upcoming election for mayor she was determined to vote for Bugsy Spittleburger, a German born second rate 'B' movie actor, whose election slogans included: ***Ban all dogs from pooping in the streets of Catmel! Humungous fines for owners of dogs that poop in the streets! We love trees – we hate poops! Keep the streets of Catmel green not brown!***

Annie had always thought that it was ridiculous for a cat to keep a dog as a pet, and she was much in favour of Spittleburger's plan to charge dog owners two thousand dollars for their dog licences.

Sheriff Chuck Smartpants had been at his desk for best part of an hour. Like his cousin Stanley he was a Birman, a Chocolate Point with warm, milk chocolate points, a pure white body and electric blue eyes.

Francesca Forensicca was sitting comfortably in his office when Annie arrived.

"Hi Fran, how you doin'?" said Annie with genuine warmth. "Nice to see you." She and Francesca had joined the Catmel Cat-PD at the same time, and had been firm friends ever since. It helped that their careers had followed parallel lines, and that they held the same rank.

"It's good to see you too, Annie," said Francesca.

"How's it bin going in the UK? What brings you back so soon?"

"Their forensic equipment is pretty basic, even worse than when we were at college! I've come back so we can use *our* equipment to establish the breed of a criminal-cat that's been committing a series of robberies. As to how it's been going, that's another story. I love the cats over there, and the Chief's cousin is a regular sort of guy, but I've been terribly homesick."

Chuck Smartpants took up the story. "I've had a word with my cousin Stanley, and explained the situation to him. He's been very understanding, but it would really help him if some other forensic cat could take over Francesca's role."

"I get it," said Annie. "You want me to go."

"You've guessed it." said Chuck. "Would you mind?"

"Heck no, I'd love to go. As a matter of fact I was so jealous when you asked Francesca to go over there. Yeah, Chief. I'd love to." Annie was crazy about wearing pearl necklaces, whether she was at work or at play, and today she had two round her neck. One was much longer than the other, and she swung it round as if it were a hula hoop. "Wow! This is really cool. Me, going to England. Awesome!" She swung the pearl necklace round and round her neck, faster and faster. Apple Pie Annie was a real cool swinger.

"That's great," said Chuck happily. "I'll give Stanley a call and tell him the good news. You'll have to keep your prankster activities in check, though."

Annie grinned. "Difficult to promise that, Chief, fresh blood over there an' all. And specially after the other night. It was a real blast!"

"What happened the other night?" asked Francesca, her curiosity aroused.

"Annie invited a few of us to dinner, if you could call it a dinner!"

"Well I *love* flowers," said Annie defensively. "You know that, Chief."

"Just because you're always running round the fields smelling flowers ....."

Francesca interrupted in frustration. "What

happened?"

"You could say we had an unusual meal," said Chuck. "Nobody realised what was going on at first. We started with soup. It looked odd, a sort of pale yellow colour, and most of us thought it tasted a bit odd, but nobody said anything. We discovered later that it was what Annie called cream of daffodil soup. She'd made it with mashed daffodils!"

"I bet it was yummy," said Francesca with a straight face.

"Not exactly," said Chuck. "When it was followed by lilies on toast, several of us were suspicious. But Annie told us they were a new type of wild mushrooms, so we ate them. The toast was all right. The main course was a disgusting stew of flowers and bulbs. It was awful, but Annie couldn't stop laughing, and refused to tell us what was in it. Until we'd got to the end."

"I'm surprised you ate it at all," said Francesca.

"We figured Annie was just a terrible cook, and didn't want to be rude."

"I suppose you had dandelion wine to wash it down!" Francesca laughed.

"If only. That wouldn't have been so bad. But it was a truly awful drink made from crushed rose petals. It tasted more like what dogs do up against trees."

"Have you tasted dog's pee then, Chief?" said Francesca.

Chuck grimaced at Francesca's joke. "Very funny!"

"Did she give you a proper meal after the false flower food?"

"What do you think? Did she heck! We all had to go to Cat-Tucky Fried Chicken. And that made Annie laugh even harder."

During this exchange Annie had remained silent, her face without emotion. But the effort of keeping a straight face was finally too much for her, and she burst out laughing, rocking from side to side with pleasure. "Go on, admit it, Chief. It was serious flower fun!"

"If you love flowers so much you should be a florist-cat instead of a police-cat. Anyway, let's get down to business. Fran, you'll have to bring Annie up to speed on the case, give her the full low-down. Then you'd best work together on the question of the breed of the cat. Presumably Annie can just take over your apartment there?"

"No problem."

"I'll have to get a cat-passport, Chief," said Annie. "I've never been out of the country, so I've never needed one."

"Don't you worry about that, Annie. You and Francesca get on and sort out the forensic answers. I'll pull a few strings and get the passport rushed through. Can you drop everything and go right away, Annie?"

"No problem, Chief," she said.

"Good. I know my cousin Stanley will appreciate that. I think he's getting desperate to nail this criminal-cat."

Monday 17th July

J umping Jack and Marmalade Marmaduke were in position outside the Cat-Odeon shortly after five o'clock. They were in plain clothes, and sat in an unmarked cat-police car. Stanley had told them to be prepared for anything. Vladimir Katakov might decide to go straight home, or might decide to go into the town centre. He might go on foot or by bus. He might even take a taxi. Stanley had assumed that he wouldn't have his own car, but even that was a possibility.

On the dot of five thirty, Vladimir Katakov emerged from the Cat-Odeon. He seemed to be in a hurry, and walked briskly in the direction of the town centre. Jack and Marmaduke got out of their car and followed. It was a bright summer's afternoon, and the sun shone warmly still. They followed him into the centre of the town. As they approached the level crossing the red lights flashed. Jack and Marmaduke were a hundred metres or so behind Vladimir, and Jack was immediately concerned that Vladimir might get across to the other side of the railway track before the gates were fully lowered. But luck was on their side, and he was forced to wait. Within a minute or two a passenger train rumbled slowly past. Jack could see that it was full of eager holiday-maker cats, many of them craning their necks to look out of the windows. They were the latest group of cats arriving in Cat-Haven-on-Sea for their annual holidays.

Once the train had gone, the gates lifted and they were on their way. At the traffic lights up ahead Vladimir turned right, and went into the Tesco-cat supermarket. Jack and Marmaduke hesitated for a few moments.

"Am I right in thinking this is the only way in and out?" said Jack.

"Yes," said Marmaduke. "We may as well wait for him here."

Twenty minutes later Vladimir emerged, carrying two carrier bags laden with food. He set off towards Cat-Haven Park, with Jack and Marmaduke not far behind. They passed the park and turned into a shabby road that led steeply uphill. Vladimir stopped outside a small terraced house with no front garden. He opened the door with a key and went inside. Jack and Marmaduke walked on past the house, noting the number, and continued uphill for fifty metres or so.

They crossed the road and stood beneath a lamppost, considering their next move.

"How long shall we give it?" said Marmaduke.

"Stanley said we should use our own judgement. We've no way of knowing whether he's going to come out again, or whether he's staying in for the night. Let's give it an hour or so. If nothing else happens at least we've got the address."

Jack checked his watch. It was just after seven thirty. "We may as well go, Marmy. No point in hanging around all night." At that very moment the door of the terraced house opened and five cats spilled out into the street. They were all Russian Blues, and incredibly they were all wearing heavy gold jewellery.

"Jumping Jellybeans!" exclaimed Jack. "Isn't that Beastly Boris?"

Marmaduke stared hard down the street. "Which one are you looking at?"

"The cat wearing the light blue shirt. I'm sure that's Boris."

"You could be right. Let's see where they go."

The five cats set off down the road, chatting animatedly. When they stopped outside and then entered the Bling Bling Bar in the bustling town centre, Jack and Marmaduke were dismayed. It was a curious place. It was well known in Cat-Haven that this unusual establishment had unusual house rules. In order to enter, cats had to be wearing serious amounts of heavy gold jewellery on their paws and round their necks. There were two bouncer-cats, dressed in white tuxedos, who manned the door in order to make sure that this rule was followed. There were no exceptions. Simply everyone had to be sporting their fair share of bling if they wanted to enter the bar. Needless to say, Jack and Marmaduke did not qualify. Their plain clothes were of course completely plain, and they were wearing no jewellery of any sort. `

"My apartment's just round the corner," said Jack. "I'll slip back there and pick up enough jewellery for both of us."

"I didn't know you were into bling, Jackster."

Jack grinned. "Well you do now. You wait here. If they come out again, call me on the mobile."

Within fifteen minutes Jack was back, with an assortment of heavy gold rings and chunky gold chains.

"My, my, Jack," said Marmaduke with a smirk on his face. "So much bling!"

"It's cool, Marmy. And it gets us into the bar."

"Have you been here before?"

"A few times. Come on, get 'dressed', and let's go." Jack gave Marmaduke a selection of jewellery, and they crossed the street. They were waved in to the bar without a problem. It was fairly dark inside, but that didn't present any problem to the sharp-eyed police-cats. They saw the group of Russian Blues, which had now increased to eight cats, on the far side of the bar. They were sitting at a large square table, playing cards, and they were all drinking vodka. There was much laughter and shouting, and waving of paws. They were a pretty noisy group, but clearly comfortable in their surroundings.

A waitress-cat went over to their table to take an order for more drinks. She leaned forward and gave one of them a kiss on the cheek, much to the amusement of his companions.

Jack decided to pay a visit to the gentlecats toilet, and contrived to pass in front of the group of Russian Blues. One of them looked over his shoulder, and straight at Jack, but without any hint of concern. Jack strode on, seemingly unaware of the Russian Blue's presence, but his keen detective eyes took in the whole scene. He couldn't believe his luck. He clearly saw that the Russian Blue had a piece missing from his right ear. "Bingo!" he said to himself as he walked on towards the toilet.

"It's definitely Boris," he said to Marmaduke as soon as he returned to their table. "When I was at the Skating Rink with Stan, Katie told us that Boris, or Yuri Katakov the Olympic skater, has a piece missing from his right ear. Did you see that cat looking at me as I walked past? *He* had a piece missing from his right ear. It's Boris, or Yuri Katakov, or whatever he calls himself."

"What a result!" exclaimed Marmaduke. "Stan

will be pleased."

There was a sudden commotion in the group of Russian Blues. One of them was on his feet, gesticulating wildly at one of his companions. He threw his cards down on the table, and miaowed furiously.

"I think he's accusing his companion of cheating," said Jack.

With lightning speed the cat on his feet drew a knife from his belt. The wicked steel blade glinted alarmingly in the overhead light. He held the knife in a threatening gesture above his head, and seemed to be on the verge of attacking one of his companions. Boris grasped the cat's paw, and spoke softly and urgently in his ear. It was clear from the aggressor-cat's body language that he was in awe of Boris, and respectfully put his knife away. The problem had been avoided, and within seconds they were all laughing and toasting each other with their glasses of vodka.

While this scene was unfolding Jack took out his mobile phone. Cleverly he took several photographs of Boris whilst pretending to write a text message.

"That was an interesting little situation, Jack. I think you were probably right about the cheating thing."

"Did you see how at ease Boris looked, Marmy? And he's obviously an important member of the group. Come on, let's go. We're finished here. And I can't wait to tell the Sarge about Beastly Boris."

Monday 17th July

S tanley had invited Peaches to accompany him to the Magyar Palace Hungarian restaurant. He had thought for quite a long time about what he should wear. Finally he had chosen blue designer jeans with fashionably cut holes at the knees, and a bright lime green t-shirt. He looked very cool indeed. Peaches was wearing a simple white cotton dress.

They arrived at the restaurant shortly after eight o'clock, and were shown to the only vacant table by a waitress-cat wearing what Stanley assumed was a traditional Hungarian folk costume. It was a cosy restaurant, warmly lit, with a small stage at the far end. The walls were decorated with old musical instruments. Stanley recognised the zither and the bagpipes, and obvious things like flutes, recorders and drums, but there were many he had never seen before. The restaurant was full, and there was an animated, excited buzz of conversation that reminded Stanley of a continental European café.

Spit and Polish, or Laszlo Kiss to give him his real name, was nowhere to be seen.

They started with a beef goulash soup, spicy and piping hot, served with chunks of roughly cut bread. There was a sudden sprinkling of applause as three male cats appeared, dressed in traditional style. Laszlo Kiss was one of them. Each one of them carried a musical instrument, and went over to the stage on which there were three chairs. They all sat down. One cat had a violin, the second a clarinet, and Laszlo had a hurdy-gurdy strapped to his midriff. After a few moments tuning their instruments, they began to play a traditional Hungarian folk dance. The musician-cats were enthusiastic, the music was lively and the diners appreciative.

Peaches pointed at Laszlo "That's a curious instrument that cat's playing."

"It's called a hurdy-gurdy," said Stanley

"At first I wondered why he had it strapped to his body, but now I understand." Laszlo needed both paws to play the instrument, cranking the handle with his right, and pressing the sliding melody keys with his left. "I'm surprised he can play at all with all those gold rings on his claws. He'd be a great success playing in the Bling Bling Bar!"

Stanley laughed. "He's the cat we're interested in. We've been watching him."

"Are you going to question him?"

"I'll ask him over to our table for a drink when they have a break."

Their main course arrived. It was rice-stuffed cabbage with sauerkraut, sausage and smoked bacon. "This smells good," said Peaches. The waitress-cat returned with a bottle of Bull's Blood red wine and invited Stanley to taste it.

"Excellent," he said after swilling it round his mouth.

They ate in silence for a while, enjoying the food, the wine and the music. Without warning, at the table next to them, a Red Shaded Turkish Angora jumped up out of her chair. She had a fine, silky coat and an elegant appearance, and she stood patiently at the side of the table. Her dining companions picked up their wine glasses and the waitress-cat removed the tablecloth. The table was now completely clear. An excited buzz of expectant miaows zipped around the restaurant, gathering momentum. It seemed that most of the cats there knew what was going to happen. The eyes of the musician-cats gleamed with the excitement of anticipation.

"Come on, Annuska!" someone shouted.

Annuska leaped onto the table and started to dance. At first her movements were slow and graceful, and she swished her gorgeously fluffy tail regally. But the mood soon changed, and she began to dance faster and faster. The three Hungarian musicians had to work overtime to keep pace with her. Her feet were flying now, criss-crossing the table. Her eyes shone with passion. She threw back her head in exaggerated fashion, and swished her tail dramatically. She was completely taken over by the music, and she danced wildly. Her feet were a blur, and it seemed a certainty that she would fall at any moment.

By now the whole restaurant, including Stanley and Peaches, was caught up in the thrilling performance. The violinist-cat was on his feet, and his bow was racing across the strings of his violin with frightening speed. The clarinetist-cat was also on his feet, and beads of sweat were pouring from his forehead. Only Laszlo remained seated, but he too was sweating. Finally the performance and the music reached a crescendo, and almost all the cats in the restaurant were on their feet, clapping wildly. After a final dizzying flourish of feet, paws and tail, Annuska jumped ten feet in the air, and performed a double somersault with twists on the way down, landing perfectly in her chair. Every single cat in the restaurant clapped and cheered, and Annuska was forced by her companions to climb back onto the table and take a bow.

"Wow!" said Peaches, her face shining with emotion. "I've never seen anything like it. That was absolutely awesome!"

Stanley took out a handkerchief from his pocket and wiped his brow. "Sensational," he exclaimed. "That was soooo cool!"

The exhausted musicians left the stage for a well deserved break. As the hubbub of excited chatter subsided, the waitress-cat brought over coffee and chestnut cake to Stanley and Peaches' table.

"Would you ask the hurdy-gurdy player to come and join us in a glass of wine?" Stanley asked her.

She went over to Laszlo, spoke softly to him and gestured in Stanley's direction. Laszlo looked over towards him, and after a few moments' thought, limped over to their table. Stanley's eyes narrowed. Laszlo hadn't appeared to limp when he had first walked over to the stage.

"Do sit down," said Stanley pleasantly, pouring a glass of wine. "You play the hurdy-gurdy so well. Where did you learn it?"

Laszlo smiled, showing a mouthful of gold-capped teeth. "In Budapest. My uncle was a famous hurdy-gurdy player, and he taught me. Pity he's no longer with us. He would have loved to see me play like that. He would have been proud of me."

Stanley switched off his friendly smile. "I have a few questions to ask you, Laszlo," he said, producing his warrant card. "I'm Detective Sergeant Smartpants of the Cat-Haven Cat-Police."

In the act of raising the glass of wine to his lips, Laszlo froze for a split second, and then he put it down, untouched. Stanley appeared not to notice the worried look on Laszlo's face, or his indecision with the wine. "We're investigating a number of robberies that have taken place in Cat-Haven over the past ten days or so. We know that you work as a cleaner-cat at the Cat-Odeon, the Skating Rink and the Kitty Kat Ice Cream Parlour. I'm sure you know that all three of them have been robbed."

Laszlo said nothing.

"We know for a fact, that a blue-haired cat committed the crimes. Tell me, Laszlo, where were you at seven o'clock this morning?"

Laszlo swallowed hard, and a guilty look momentarily crossed his face. "I ... er ... was at home," he said unconvincingly.

"Can anyone confirm that?"

"Er ... no, I was on my own."

"What were you doing?"

"Sleeping."

"What time did you go to bed?"

"About five o'clock."

"Why so late?"

"I was cleaning the Cat-Odeon."

"What time did you finish?"

"About half past four."

"Are you sure about that?"

"Pretty much."

"Did you go to Torcat beach where the fishercats bring their boats ashore?"

There was a look of complete shock on Laszlo's face.

"You did, didn't you?" probed Stanley.

"No," said Laszlo firmly.

"What's wrong with your foot?"

The question puzzled Laszlo. "What do you mean?"

"You limped over to our table just now."

"Oh, just a bit of cramp. I often get it when I've been sitting down playing the hurdy-gurdy for a while."

"Have you been to the Feline Furniture Emporium recently?"

Laszlo hesitated. "Er … no."

"When was the last time you were there?"

"I don't remember … maybe two months ago."

"Why did you go there?"

"To buy a bed."

"Did you go there last week?"

"No, I just said. The last time I was there was two months ago."

"Okay, Laszlo, that'll be all for now. I may want to see you again, though."

"Excuse me for a moment, Stan," said Peaches. "I'm just going to the cat-ladies." She got to her feet.

Laszlo looked relieved, and got up from the table, his glass of wine still untouched. As he turned away, Peaches stumbled and put her paw on his arm to steady herself.

"Sorry," she said.

Laszlo stared at her coldly, and walked over to re-join his companions. There was no trace of a limp.

When Peaches returned from the toilet she gave Stanley a small plastic bag. It contained the blue hair that she had plucked from Laszlo's arm.

"Good girl," said Stanley with satisfaction, and pocketed the plastic bag.

"I wasn't sure I'd be able to do it."

"If I may say so, my dear Peaches, you carried out my instructions perfectly. Are you sure you never went to cat-police training school?"

Peaches laughed. But she also blushed.

"What did you make of Laszlo, Peaches?"

"I think he was lying about being in bed at seven o'clock this morning. And about going down to the beach."

"Yes, so do I."

"Did something happen at the beach early this morning?"

"One of the fishercats was hit on the head as she was pulling her boat up onto the beach. A dozen or so mackerel were stolen from her."

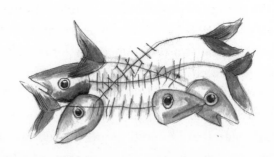

Tuesday 18th July

All the cat-constables and cadet-cats of the Cat-Haven Cat-Police were assembled in the Crime Room. Stanley Smartpants had called a meeting for nine o'clock sharp.

"The Chief would like to say a few words," said Stanley.

"Thank you, Stan," said Derek. "I'd like you all to re-double your efforts in our attempt to apprehend the criminal-cat responsible for the 'Mackerel Robberies'."

"He's havin' a laugh, Jack," said Marmaduke, shielding his mouth with his paw. "How can we re-double our efforts, when we haven't even doubled them in the first place!" Jack laughed.

Derek looked in Jack's direction, but said nothing. "There have been two more incidents since the last meeting, and it's a matter of the utmost urgency that we apprehend the criminal-cat responsible.

I'm under pressure from the mayor to get this case brought to a conclusion. He's been getting complaints from businesscats in Cat-Haven, and some of them are threatening to hold back payment of their rates. We *must* get this resolved, cats. Over to you, Stan."

"Thank you, Chief." Stanley walked over to the Incident Board. The robbery at the Feline Furniture Store, and the theft of Harriet Fishnet's mackerel had been added to the list of crimes. "As I'm sure you all know already, Jack and Marmaduke spotted Beastly Boris in the Bling Bling Bar last night. So he's right back at the top of our list of suspects. Before we discuss what we're going to do about him we'll just update you all on the other potential suspects. Okay, Stephen, let's hear your report on the Blue Korat, the waiter-cat at the Cluck Cluck Diner."

Studious Stephen coughed nervously. This would be only the second time he would stand up in front of his cat-colleagues to deliver a report. The first time was yesterday, when he reported on the interview with Ten Bangles Tonia. But that had been straightforward. This was a different frying pan of fish altogether. And he wasn't looking forward to it. He opened his notebook.

"Well," he said, "Pamela and I caught up with him last night. His name is Billy Blunderhead, and he works part-time as a waiter-cat at the Cluck Cluck Diner. Although the Cluck Cluck Chicken Takeaway has been around for a long time, the Diner has only been open a few weeks. The owner, Larry Cluck

Cluck, explained to us that since he'd had so much to do to get the place up and running, he hadn't had time to get all the information together on his staff."

"Yes, he told me exactly the same thing when *I* went there," said Jack.

Stanley guessed where this was probably leading. "Do we have an address for Billy Blunderhead, Stephen?"

"I'm afraid not, Sarge. He'd already gone by the time we interviewed Larry Cluck Cluck, and we sort of assumed that Cluck Cluck would have all Billy's personal details in his file." Stephen blushed furiously when he saw Stanley roll his eyes in exasperation.

"What exactly did you find out about him?"

"Not very much, Sarge. He wasn't very communicative .... and he left soon after we arrived."

"You should have made him wait while you interviewed Cluck Cluck," said Derek.

"It's easy for you to say that, Chief. But the fact of the matter is it's not so easy when you're out there in the field, so to speak."

"I hear what you say Stephen, but it's nonsense. You have to be prepared for these things. Didn't they teach you that in college?"

Stephen blushed furiously.

"Did you at least come back with one of his hairs?" asked Stanley

"I'm sorry, Sarge. We just didn't have the opportunity. He .... sort of ...."

Pamela jumped in to try and save Stephen's blushes. "I didn't like him. My instinct tells me he's a bad 'un."

"Is there anything in particular that makes you feel that way?"

"His name is stupid for a start!" A couple of the female cadet-cats giggled. "He was terribly clumsy. He fell over his own feet twice in the short time we were there! When we interviewed Larry Cluck Cluck he told us that they called him Blunderhead because he's always mixing up the food orders, and taking them to the wrong customers. My guess is that he'll get kicked out before long. I don't trust him. He should be added to the list of suspects."

"Did he have a limp, Pamela?"

"No. Definitely not."

"Put him on the list, Tammy. We certainly can't eliminate him at the moment." Stanley walked over to the Incident Board as Tammy was adding Billy Blunderhead's name. "We've added another column to the suspects list to show which cats we've got a DNA sample from. This is going to be a crucial part of the case. Let's see where we've got to.

"We've removed Sing Song, Larry Cluck Cluck, and Klepto Klaws from the main list of suspects, and added Cauliflower Colin and Spit and Polish. Jack and Marmaduke interviewed Saucy Suzette, the French Chef at Chez Les Chats and she's now eliminated. So is Ten Bangles Tonia as we heard from Stephen and Pamela.

Cat-Haven Cat-Police
INCIDENT BOARD
CASE: Mackerel Robberies
SUSPECTS & OTHERS

Last updated: 18th July 2008

SUSPECTS	COLOUR/BREED	INFORMATION TO HAND	DNA
Beastly Boris aka Yuri Katakov	Russian Blue	Illegal immigrant? Did not leave the country as previously thought. Now seems to be unemployed. Regular at Bling Bling Bar	
Vladimir Katakov	Russian Blue	? brother of Yuri — Handycat at the Cat-Odeon. ? also illegal immigrant. Also regular at Bling Bling Bar	
6 Unknown Cats	All Russian Blues	By association with the Katakovs	
* Mystery Cat*	Blue-grey or silver blue Breed not known	Seen at — Cat Diamonds "R" Us, Skating Rink, Kitty Kat Ice Cream Parlour	
Cauliflower Colin	Blue Korat	Projectionist-cat at Cat-Odeon	DNA
Spit and Polish aka Laszlo Kiss	Blue Burmese	Hungarian cleaner-cat at Skating Rink, Cat-Odeon, Kitty Kat Ice Cream Parlour. Also musician-cat at Magyar Palace	DNA

Cat-Haven Cat-Police
CASE: Mackerel Robberies
SUSPECTS & OTHERS

INCIDENT BOARD

Last updated: 18th July 2008

OTHER SUSPECTS	COLOUR/BREED	INFORMATION TO HAND			
Albert Tartpincher	Blue Burmese	Window Cleaner-cat at Cat Diamonds "R" Us, Skating Rink, Cat-Odeon. Arrested over theft of pineapple tarts 6 months ago.			
Billy Blunderhead	Blue Korat	Waiter-cat at Cluck Cluck Diner			
Calculating Calvin	Russian Blue	Bookkeeper-cat at Kitty Kat Ice Cream Parlour			

"Jack, can you put up Beastly Boris' photo on the big screen. The one you took last night on your mobile." Stanley paused while Jack pressed the computer keys until Boris' photo appeared on the screen. "As you can see, he's surrounded by a large group of friends. For all we know they may be part of a Russian Mafia gang."

"I still think *he's* the criminal-cat," said Derek Dimwit to no-one in particular.

"We've either got to get him down here to the station so we can interview him, or somehow get a hair from him so we can have it analysed. Or both. In essence he's protected by the group of Russian Blues, so to arrest him we'd have to break into the house he's living in."

"Oooh! That sounds exciting," gushed Tammy. "Can I be on the team, Sarge?"

"A break-in involves too many risks. Some of our cats could get hurt. It's not the answer, Tammy."

Tammy looked disappointed, and started to preen herself. "That's so unfair. I never get to have any fun."

"The forensic evidence is the most important factor in this case. I'm sure of it. We *have* to get DNA samples from all the cats on the board."

"What have you got in mind Stan, regarding Beastly Boris?" asked Derek.

"We think that these Russian Blues are regulars at the Bling Bling Bar. Maybe they even go there every night. They were well known to all the staff. Boris also seemed to be confident that we're not looking for him any more, or at any rate he seems to be relaxed."

"I don't think he had any reason to suspect that me and Marmaduke were cat-police," said Jack, "even if he noticed us."

"Yep," said Marmaduke. "I think the cat-police are the last thing on his mind."

"It's the last thing on my mind too," said Vincent. "Sarge, I need to go for a poo."

"Yo de yo," said Jack, "he's turning into a poet ….. and he doesn't even know it! Ha! Ha! Ha!"

Vincent didn't wait for Stanley's approval. He jumped up from his chair and ran swiftly out of the room.

"OK," said Stanley, ignoring the interruption. "I think we'll post a couple of officer-cats outside the bar, suitably dripping with bling of course. When the Russian Blues turn up they can follow them in. Then, and this is the tricky bit, one of us has to engineer a situation in which we can get one of Boris' hairs."

"Maybe we could get some saliva from the glass he's drinking from?" suggested Stephen.

"You're havin' a laugh," said Marmaduke. "That's a really dumb idea. What are you going to do, Stephen? Go up to him and say … can I have your glass please? I want to see if you've left any of your spit on it!" Several of the female cadet-cats laughed noisily. They didn't like Stephen much. He was always putting them down. It was great to see him getting some of his own medicine.

Jack put the boot in. "Instead of Studious Stephen perhaps we should call him Bungalow Bonce."

"Why's that, Jackster?" said Marmaduke, playing along.

"Cos he's got nothing upstairs! Ha! Ha! Ha!"

The female cadet-cats were having a great time. Stephen wasn't.

Cynthia dug Tammy in the ribs. "Jack's awful, isn't he?" she said. "But he does make me laugh."

"Don't be so nasty to Stephen," said Pamela to Jack. "He's just trying to make helpful suggestions."

"I suspect that it would be more difficult to walk out of the Bling Bling Bar with a glass," said Stanley, "It'll be easier to get one of Boris' hairs. But as good police-cats we should always be aware of *all* the possibilities."

"Let me and Marmy go tonight," said Jack. "After all, we know what we're walking into."

"I'm happy with that," said Stanley. "Now, let's consider the other suspects we have on the list. Up to a point we can discount Vladimir Katakov and the other six Russian Blues since basically they're tied in with Boris. At any rate, I don't think we need to spend too much time on them at the moment."

"Stan," said Derek hesitantly. "Why has the next cat, the one that limps, got asterisks?"

Several cats laughed, and Soppy Cynthia gave a sigh of relief, for she had been about to ask the same question.

"It's because he's not a suspect in his own right, Chief. We don't know who he is. It's a fair bet that he's one of the cats that we've already got on the board. It's a question of fitting him into the jigsaw."

"I realise that, Stan. I'm not completely stupid. I just wondered about the asterisks. Carry on."

"Some of you dismissed Albert Tartpincher after our last meeting, but I think that was a mistake. Although he was never charged with anything, there is the outstanding matter of the tarts stolen from the Albert Hall. And he did have easy access to three of the crime scenes. He's a genuine suspect, and I think we need to bring him in to the station to be interviewed. At that point it will be easy to get one of his hairs for analysis."

Encouraged by Pamela's support, Stephen plucked up the courage to make another observation. "It's a well known fact that identity parades are a major weapon in the conviction of criminals."

All the cats in the Crime Room were silent, wondering where this was leading.

"During my college course they constantly stressed its importance. Why don't we get all the suspects lined up together, and call in the three witnesses?"

Jack and Marmaduke burst out laughing.

Marmaduke made no effort to conceal his contempt. "You *must* be havin' a laugh. You get more and more stupid every day, Stephen. As the Sarge has already explained, it would be almost impossible to get Beastly Boris down to the station for starters. You should have paid more attention in class, and spent less time looking down your nose at your fellow students. What you would have remembered if you had, is that the identity parade is a way of getting a witness to confirm that the cat you've got pegged for the crime *is* the villain-cat. As another piece of evidence. We don't even know who committed the crime yet. And anyway if your three witnesses each picked out a different cat, where would you be then?"

Laughter cascaded round the room, and once more Stephen blushed a bright shade of pink. The female cadet-cats were in heaven, and Jack clapped Marmaduke on the back.

"I wouldn't have put it quite like that," said Stanley, "but the basic thrust of Marmaduke's argument is correct."

There was more laughter, which Stanley hadn't intended, and Stephen's face turned even pinker.

"Let's move on to Cauliflower Colin. The Chief and I interviewed him yesterday. Personally I don't think he's the criminal-cat, although he did have access to Miserable Melvin's office."

"So did every other cat that works at the Cat-Odeon," said Derek.

"This is true," said Stanley. "At least we've got one of his hairs for analysis, so we should be able to eliminate him."

"But not until Francesca gets back," said

Marmaduke. "When *is* she due back, Sarge?"

"She's not coming back. One of her colleagues, a cat called Apple Pie Annie, is coming over in her place."

"Sounds sweet enough to eat," said Jack. The female cadet-cats laughed. "When is she coming over?"

"My cousin Chuck is going to ring me tomorrow, so I hope to know then." Stanley scratched his nose with his claws before continuing. "If you look at the Board you'll see that Spit and Polish turns out to be a musician-cat at the Magyar Palace Hungarian restaurant. I went there last night with Pretty Peaches."

Jack winked at Marmaduke, and then outrageously at the female cadet-cats, who tittered softly and gave Jack knowing looks.

"Ahem," coughed Stanley, slightly embarrassed. "He was very shifty, definitely had something to hide. Both Peaches and I thought that he lied to us about where he was yesterday morning when the mackerel were stolen from Harriet Fishnet. Curiously he also had a sort of a limp. He didn't limp when he first came out to go up to the stage, but *did* limp after he'd been sitting down for a while. It's difficult to know what to make of that. However, there's no doubt that he would have had the perfect opportunity at three of the crime scenes. After all he has access to them at night, when there's no-one around. He's *very* high on the list of suspects in my view."

Derek Dimwit looked puzzled. "Why is he near

the bottom of the list on the board then, Stan?"

"Because we've only just added him to the list, Chief. As to the question of Billy Blunderhead, we obviously need to question him again. If Pamela is right about him not lasting in the job much longer, not to mention her instinctive feeling about him, we need to organise that as soon as possible. Perhaps you and Marmaduke could do that tomorrow, Jack." Stephen blushed again, for he realised that he had been taken off the assignment. And what was worse was that every other cat knew it.

"No problem, Sarge," said Jack. "leave it to us. We'll deal with it as soon as we can."

"Let's break for lunch," said Stanley.

"You know Greta's off sick, don't you Sarge?" said Tammy.

"We'll have to have sandwiches or jacket potatoes or something from the bakery. Make a list of what everyone wants, and then a couple of you can go down to the bakery to buy the stuff."

"Better not send Tammy, Sarge," said Jack with a mischievous grin on his face. "Last time *she* was in a bakery ...." Tammy had a puzzled look on her face. She had no idea where this was leading. "....... she got fed up of waiting in the queue, so she lay down on the floor and fell asleep. A few minutes later the baker-cat came into the shop carrying a large freshly baked chocolate cake. It smelled so good it woke Tammy up. Ha! Ha! Ha!"

Tammy smiled happily, for she enjoyed the joke as much as everyone else. And it was well known amongst the cats of the Cat-Haven cat-police that Tammy would go anywhere, and do anything, for a piece of chocolate cake.

"The last time I was in the bakery," said Jack, "the cat in front of me in the queue asked for a pastry from the window. When the assistant-cat reached into the window to get it, she got an electric shock and pulled back her paw in double quick time. And I said to the old lady-cat in front of me … you know why she got an electric shock, don't you? She shook her head, and I said ……." Jack paused for ages ….. "it's because there are so many currant buns in the window! Ha! Ha! Ha!"

The punch line was greeted with a generous number of laughs, and Jack looked very pleased with himself.

"I wonder what's happened to Vinnie?" said Pamela. "He should have been back by now."

"Oh, yeah, I'd forgotten about him," said Tammy.

Stanley held up his hand, and all his cats just knew that a poem was coming. There was an expectant hush.

> *"When Vinnie runs off to go for a poo,*
> *Of how long he needs we haven't a clue.*
> *As long as it takes, he thinks he can stay,*

Safe in the knowledge it will be OK.
But I tell you quite straight, I do have a hunch,
That he'll dally too long, and miss out on lunch!"

"Good one, Sarge," shouted out Jack. Most of the cats in the Crime Room laughed out loud. Everyone enjoyed the send-up of Vinnie.

Marmaduke patted his stomach. "Maybe it wouldn't be a bad idea if he *did* miss out on lunch," he said drily.

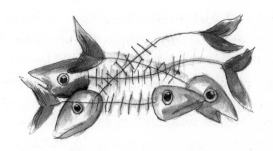

Tuesday 18th July

Jack and Marmaduke arrived at the Bling Bling Bar shortly before seven o'clock. Two cadet-cats had been on duty outside the bar since six, and reported that there had been no sign of the Russian Blues. Jack and Marmaduke had decided in advance that they would wait until nine o'clock, and settled down in the unmarked cat-police car that was parked across the street. They were both heavily 'blinged up', Jack in particular. He was wearing three chunky gold chains round his neck, and a gold ring on every one of the eight claws of his front paws. Extraordinarily he also had diamond studs in both his ears. The only things he didn't have, thought Marmaduke, were a ring in the nose and a stud in his tongue. Marmaduke told him that he had overdone it, but Jack just grinned happily.

In the event they had to wait no more than a few minutes. The same group of five Russian Blues arrived laughing and joking, obviously in high spirits. They were greeted in friendly fashion by the bouncers, and went straight in to the bar.

Jack and Marmaduke gave them time to settle, and followed them in five minutes later. The Russian Blues were sitting at the same large table, and there was the same group of eight males, but they had been joined by four females. The males were playing cards, while the females sat chatting to each other.

Jack and Marmaduke strolled slowly up to the bar, giving themselves plenty of time to work out where would be the best place to sit. A terribly pretty Russian Blue waitress-cat was behind the bar. She was quite tall and her short, dense coat of bright blue was tipped with a silvery sheen. Her eyes were a vivid green, and she smiled brightly at them.

Marmaduke took an instant fancy to her. "What's your name?" he asked.

"Vodka Valentina," she said, making eye contact with him.

"Is that because you drink too much vodka?" asked Jack.

Valentina laughed, showing her perfect white teeth. "No, it is because I am not drinking any alcohol always."

"What do you do when you're not serving drinks in here?" said Marmaduke.

"I am student-cat. I am studying the English cat-lingo at the Cat-Haven College."

"Good luck with it." Marmaduke smiled. "I'll have a pint of lime and lemonade with lots of ice please, Valentina."

"Orange juice for me," said Jack.

As Valentina gave them their change, Marmaduke became a little bolder. "And what do you do in your free time?"

"I like to have a rest in nature with my friends."

Marmaduke nodded. "I see." He couldn't think of anything else to say.

They chose a table that gave them a good view of the Russian Blues, but one that was not too close.

"What do you think she meant by that, Marmy?" said Jack.

"I dunno. I guess she likes being out of doors, in the fields and woods, and by the sea perhaps."

"Not water sports or playing games, you mean? Are you going to ask her out on a date?"

"Maybe. That reminds me, I forgot to ask you yesterday, how was your date with Gloria on Sunday night?"

Jack smiled a thin smile. "It was good."

"Is that all?"

"Well …. it was good."

"What did you do?"

"We went down to the beach, and walked along the sands and the cliff top path right up to Torcat. We stopped off for a drink in The Cat's Whiskers pub on the sea front. Then we walked back and went for fish and chips in the Sea View Restaurant, you know where I witnessed the necklace exchange between Klepto and Sing Song. Then we went to a disco."

"So you took her to a top restaurant? No expense spared."

"It was her idea actually. It was really good fish and chips. It would be a good place for you to take Valentina. You know, traditional British fish and chips. And not too taxing on the pocket."

"Are you taking her out again?"

"Maybe."

They had been there for quite a while sipping their drinks, when Valentina came over to their table. "You like more drinks?" she said.

Before either of them could respond, a huge and very ugly ginger tom cat came up behind Valentina. He put a paw on her shoulder.

Valentina turned round and as soon as she saw the ginger tom, and the leering look on his face, she cried out. "Take away the paw."

The ginger tom grinned an ugly grin. "Don't be like that," he said strengthening his grip on her shoulder. "I just want to buy you a drink."

"Get off," Valentina hissed. "I don't want."

Marmaduke jumped up from his chair, and put a restraining paw on the ginger tom. "Leave the young lady-cat alone. She doesn't want you pawing her."

"What's it got to do with you?" said the ginger tom aggressively.

Marmaduke tried to take the heat out of the situation. "Come on now, there's a good chap."

Without warning the ginger tom lashed out at Marmaduke. On one of the middle claws of his right paw he was wearing a huge, knobby, gold ring. It was more like a dangerous weapon than a piece of jewellery. He smashed his fist into Marmaduke's face, and caught him flush on the nose and mouth. Marmaduke fell down instantly, clutching his bloodied nose and lips.

This scene lasted no more than a few seconds. As it unfolded Boris and three other Russian Blues got up from their seats and raced across the bar. Boris was the first to get there. He grabbed the ginger tom by the throat, and jerked his head backwards. The ginger tom let out a squeal of pain. Boris kneed him in the stomach and then landed a hammer blow to the head. The ginger tom staggered backwards. When he saw another three Russian Blues running towards him, he turned and ran away.

Jack was already comforting Valentina, and sat her down on a chair. Two of the Russian Blues helped Marmaduke up.

"You don't look good," said Boris, as Marmaduke struggled to his feet. "Sergei," he said addressing one of his companions, "go for water and clean cloth so we can bathe this guy's wounds. Are you OK, Valentina?"

"I'm fine," she said. "Thanks to this lovely cat!"

Despite his bruised and bloodied lips Marmaduke attempted a smile.

"Valentina is my sister," said Boris. The resemblance was clear. Like his sister, Boris had a dense, silvery blue coat and vivid green eyes. He too was tall and he had a presence about him that suggested that he was a leader. "I am very protective to her," he said. "I am very grateful that you helping her. You must come to join our table and take glass of vodka."

Jack instantly realised that the opportunity they had been waiting for had presented itself in a most unexpected way. He looked at Marmaduke and saw from the expression in his eyes that he too appreciated their good fortune.

"Come, Valentina, you too must take the vodka. It is your time. It is necessary. And it will mean that you live up to your name." Boris' face creased into a thousand smiles.

"OK, brother. I do as you ask."

Boris helped Valentina to her feet, and they all went over to the large table, where the others had already created some space. Before they sat down Boris turned to Marmaduke once more. "I am Yuri." He held out his paw. "It is pleasure in meeting you. And this is my brother Vladimir."

"I'm Marmaduke."

"And I'm Jack."

"Good," said Yuri.

****

The card game was abandoned, and Marmaduke was the centre of attention. Many of the Russian Blues made nice comments:

"Thank you so much."

"You very kind."

"You are brave cat."

Valentina beamed, and looked deep into Marmaduke's eyes. "Thank you so very much, Mar … mee … dook."

Marmaduke laughed. "Just call me Marmy," he said.

Yuri poured out three large measures of vodka, and Vladimir re-filled everyone's glass. "I am making the toast. To Mar…mee, our new and forever friend."

"To Mar…mee!" Every one of the Russian Blues said this at the same time. They downed their vodkas in one.

"It is best to take in the one swallow," said Yuri.

Valentina and Jack raised their glasses. Marmaduke looked a little uncertain. "I'm not sure if I should toast myself."

"Of course you should. And remember, in the one swallow."

They all drank their vodkas down in one mouthful. Valentina started coughing furiously. Most of the Russian Blues, including Yuri, laughed.

After her coughing fit had ended Valentina smiled. "Is very warm down here," she said rubbing her throat and chest. "My head feel funny." There was more laughter.

Yuri poured another shot of vodka for Jack and Marmaduke, who knew that they really had no choice but to accept. Valentina put her paw over her glass.

"No thank you, brother. I have to return to working. I am fine now. Is there something I get you, Mar...mee?"

Marmaduke hesitated, and then said. "If it's not too much trouble, I'd love some toast and marmalade." He looked a little sheepish.

Valentina laughed. "This is amazing," she said. "I am having the toast and marmalade for breakfast every morning. I love so much. I bring it to you immediately now." She got up from the table. Marmaduke also stood. Valentina put out her paw, and Marmaduke took it eagerly. It was soft and warm to the touch.

"Thank you again so much," she said. "I am hoping we meet again soon. I would like to know you closer. You must know I am serious cat when situation calls for it. I dream some cat to steal my heart one day. You can come here any time and I buy you drink." She looked deep into his eyes.

Marmaduke blushed. "I *will* come back to see you Valentina."

"I should think so," said Jack. "Who could resist a free drink?" There was more laughter around the table.

Yuri, who was sitting next to Jack, clapped him on the back. "Good one, my friend."

"Thank you," said Jack, touching Yuri lightly. As he did so, he pulled a short blue hair from the Russian's shoulder. He stood up. "Excuse me, I must go to the toilet." He left the table, and walked over to the gentlecats toilet. He used the opportunity to deposit the blue hair safely in a plastic bag.

Jack and Marmaduke spent another hour with their new Russian friends. Before finally getting up to leave.

Yuri was on his feet instantly. "I thank you from bottom of my heart for looking out for my sister. You will always be my friend, now and forever. Here," he said, fishing something out of his pocket. "These are two tickets for big Russian ice show that is on at Cat-Haven Empire at end of next month. We only just signed contract for show few days ago. Me and my friends here, we are all ice skaters."

Momentarily Jack was uncertain. He wasn't sure whether or not to mention his sister. He decided that it would be better if he did, since it might seem odd later if he didn't. He knew of course that Yuri was the Olympic champion, and that he had skated with Katie recently. But this was information he could not have known from their conversation this evening. "That's a coincidence. My sister's a famous ice skater. I don't know if you've ever heard of her, Skatie Katie."

"Of course I have. I know her just little. We skated together about ten days ago."

"Small world," said Jack.

Yuri grasped Marmaduke in a bear hug. And as he released him he kissed him noisily on both cheeks.

Jack and Marmaduke knew that they would have to leave the car and walk back to the station after drinking so much vodka.

Marmaduke was a little unsteady on his feet. "What did you *make* of all that, Jack? Bit of a turn up for the book."

"It does shed a new light on Boris. Or maybe we have to call him Yuri now."

"He's a really nice guy, isn't he? I do hope he's not the criminal-cat."

"It would put a bit of a damper on you dating Valentina, wouldn't it? So you *are* going to ask her out on a date, aren't you, Marmy?"

"Maybe."

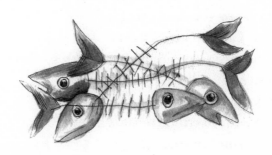

Wednesday 19th July

It was 7.00 a.m. and Stanley Smartpants was in his office early, waiting for the call he was expecting from his cousin Chuck. In California it was still Tuesday evening. Eleven p.m. to be precise.

Stanley had just made himself a cup of tea and settled down to read the Cat-Haven Chronicle when the phone rang, piercing the silence of the empty office.

"Hey, Stanley," came a familiar voice down the phone. "How you doin', buddy?"

"Hey, Chuck, how *you* doin'?"

"Stop teasin' me. You know that's so cheesy. You Brits just can't pull off a Yankie accent!"

"OK, you win. Have you got any news for me?"

"Sure. You're criminal-cat is a blue Burmese."

"How sure are you?"

"One hundred per cent. Francesca and Annie worked on it together, and came up with a definite result just before seven o'clock this evening."

"That's great. It really narrows down our search."

"You've gotta get yourselves one of these machines, Stan. We couldn't do anything without it. As long as you can get DNA evidence, it allows you to eliminate a bunch of suspects. Makes cat-crime fighting so much easier."

"I'm sure you're right. Can you fax me the details of the machine *you've* got, where you bought it, and how much it cost?"

"Sure. It's expensive though, I can tell you that. In fact, if you don't mind me borrowing your word, it cost squintillions of dollars."

They both tried to speak at once, the difficulties of the long distance telephone delay coming into play. Finally Chuck paused long enough for Stanley to be heard without interruption.

"What's the news on Apple Pie Annie? Any idea yet when she's coming over?"

"Yep. She's leaving from San Francisco tomorrow evening. She'll be arriving at Heathcat early on Thursday morning, about 6.00 a.m. your time."

"Great! I really appreciate this, Chuck. If you see her before she sets off, tell her I'm very grateful that she's coming over at such short notice."

"You're welcome. And no worries, I'll pass on your message to her. She's a great girl, but there is one thing I haven't told you about her. She's a prankster. So watch your back!"

Stanley laughed. "I think we can handle that, Chuck. We're pretty laid back over here. We've got some entertaining characters, and we do like a laugh."

"Yeah, Francesca told me. I heard some of your stories. But I still say …. watch your back!"

Stanley had called a meeting of all his cats for nine o'clock. Since he had plenty of time in hand he thought he would go down to the sea front. He lived near the harbour, and often had breakfast at the Sea View Café, which opened early for the fishercats and working cats. He chose to park his car at home and walk the few hundred metres along the seashore to the Café. It would stimulate his appetite.

"Good morning, Stanley," said the manageress-cat. "What can I get for you? Your usual?"

"Yes please Wanda," said Stanley, and went over to sit at a window table. He had brought his copy of the Cat-Haven Chronicle with him to do the crossword over breakfast.

When his breakfast was put in front of him he looked at it with eager anticipation. There were two fried eggs, two sausages, two rashers of crispy bacon, tomatoes, mushrooms, baked beans and sautéed potatoes, two slices of toast and butter, and a mug of steaming hot tea.

"Now that's what I call an English breakfast! That is sooo cool!" he said to himself, and tucked in with relish.

Shortly after he had finished breakfast he noticed that there was a blue Burmese sitting at another table. He had been so engrossed in his meal, not to mention the crossword, that he had not seen the cat arrive. He thought about going over to him to ask him a few questions, but decided that he was being foolish. There were squintillions of blue Burmese in Cat-Haven, and he had no reason to interrogate this particular cat.

Driving back to the station, Stanley couldn't get it out of his mind that he had seen the Burmese before. But he just couldn't remember where or when.

Everyone was assembled in the Crime Room. They all knew that Stanley had been hoping to speak to his cousin in California.

"Good morning everyone. I'll come straight to the point. Our criminal-cat is a blue Burmese."

There were several gasps from around the room.

"So it's not Beastly Boris after all," said Derek Dimwit in shocked surprise.

Marmaduke had a broad smile on his face, and Jack gave him an encouraging wink.

"That's right, Chief. And it also knocks out Vladimir Katakov, Cauliflower Colin, and Billy Blunderhead, not to mention Calculating Calvin."

Stephen sighed with relief, after the mess he'd

made of the Billy Blunderhead interview. Marmaduke thought of making a sarcastic comment directed at Stephen. But he was in too generous a mood to bother. He was much too pleased that Valentina's brother and his new friends from last night were off the hook.

"We now have only two suspects," said Stanley, "Albert Tartpincher and Laszlo Kiss. That might be *good* news, in that we only need to concentrate on two cats. Or it might be *bad* news, since if the criminal-cat isn't one of them, we're back to square one. Our new forensic-cat, Apple Pie Annie, is due to arrive at Heathcat from California tomorrow morning. Tammy, I'd like you to go and collect her."

Tammy looked really pleased. "Of course, Sarge," she said happily. But she hadn't considered the consequences.

"Greta will give you the flight details. I think it's best if you drive up today and spend the night in a hotel at Heathcat. You'll still need an early start tomorrow, but at least you'll be on the spot, and it breaks the journey in two. Annie will need to rest after her journey, so I want you to take her straight to Francesca's apartment. If you ring in to the office when you're an hour away, Charlie will organise one of the cadet-cats to meet you there."

The expression on Tammy's face had changed. The smiles were gone, as she contemplated the gruelling journeys ahead, but she said nothing.

****

"The most pressing thing for Annie to do on Friday," continued Stanley, "will be to carry out a DNA comparison of the hair sample we have from Laszlo Kiss with those found at the various crime scenes. As a matter of urgency we need one from Albert Tartpincher as well. I want to interview both these cats here in the station. Albert Tartpincher has been a little bit of a low priority so far, and in a way that's my fault. I still think that he's unlikely to be the criminal-cat. However, he's suddenly become a higher priority.

"I've rung Skatie Katie, and she told me that Tartpincher is due to clean the windows at the Skating Rink tomorrow. He usually does them in the morning. Stephen, I want you and Pamela to be at the Skating Rink at nine o'clock tomorrow morning, arrest him the moment you see him, and bring him in.

"I want Laszlo Kiss in here tomorrow as well. Jack, I want you and Marmaduke to call on him early doors tomorrow morning. I'd rather not risk alerting him to our interest, so I don't want us to ask around to establish his movements. Get to his house for seven o'clock tomorrow morning, and just wait for him."

Marmaduke groaned audibly and Jack nudged him in the ribs.

"Sorry to disturb your beauty sleep, Marmaduke," said Stanley, "but we are the Cat-Haven cat-police. Let me just say this to you."

Every cat sat forward expectantly.

"To catch the cats that rob and steal,
There is no time to groan and squeal.
The cat that does commit the crime,
He does not care about the time.
So oft to solve the blinking crime,
It's out of bed you have to climb.
Now let me tell you off the cuff,
Our Tammy has it much more tough.
But did you hear that she was moaning?
Even though she'll lose a lot of sleep,
There was not heard a single peep,
So shut your mouth and quit your groaning!"

Stanley's poem was greeted with much applause. No-one clapped louder and more heartily than Tammy. The smiles had returned to her face.

Marmaduke smiled too. "Good one, Sarge. Point taken."

The meeting broke up and Stanley went back to his office. Derek followed him in.

"That was a good result, Stan, even if it does mean I was wrong about Beastly Boris."

"I may turn out to be wrong about Albert Tartpincher, Chief. It's the police-cat hazard."

Derek looked puzzled. "I hear what you say, Stan, but what do you mean? What's the police-cat hazard?"

"Being wrong."

Friday 21st July

Tammy had arranged to collect Apple Pie Annie from her apartment at eight o'clock in the morning. "How are you feeling?" she asked.

Annie smiled. "Better than I expected. Actually I slept pretty well on the plane, and as you know, a bit in your car. I managed to stay up till ten o'clock, which I thought was pretty good. But I was wide awake by four o'clock this morning."

"I've never been abroad before, so I don't know what this jet lag business is all about."

"It's my first time travelling abroad too, so I can't say I know anything about it either. I know that you're all waiting on me and my analysis. Let's hope I manage to stay awake long enough to get it done."

"Good to have you on board, Annie," said Stanley. "We really appreciate your coming over at such short notice. And starting work before you've had a proper chance to get over the jet lag."

"Thanks, Chief. I'm wide awake, and raring to go."

"I'm not actually the Chief, Annie. I'm like second in charge. Mostly, everyone calls me Sarge. But I think you should call me Stan." Stanley picked up the office phone. "Greta, I'd like you to come up to my office. I want to introduce you to Annie." He put the phone down. "In many ways Greta is the most important person here, although it would never do to let her know that. She likes to feel that she's some kind of martyr. Likes to have a good old moan about how much she's got to do, and how much we all take her for granted. Which of course we do! But she's a really genuine cat, with a heart of gold."

"What *does* she do then?"

"She's the station cook. And she's also the secretary."

"I can guess how she must feel about that!"

Stanley shrugged his shoulders. "I know. It is too much for her sometimes. Mostly she gets her work from me. Would you like to know what she calls herself?

"Sure. Lay it on me."

"She likes to call herself the chief assistant to the assistant chief!"

"I like that."

There was a light knock at the door and Greta

breezed through it, singing happily. "Hello Annie," she said. "Nice to meet you. Come with me and I'll give you a tour of the whole place, and show you where the forensic lab is. I'll fix you a nice breakfast too. You must be starving."

Annie raised her eyebrows and looked at Stanley pointedly. "I think I'm going to like working here."

"Before you go Annie, I want to give you our samples for analysis."

"How many have you got?"

"Well, at the moment we've only got one. When the call came through from Chuck, telling us that the criminal-cat is a blue Burmese, it left us with just two main suspects. We have a hair from one of them." Stanley got up from his desk and padded over to the cupboard that stood against the far wall.

"I love your pants, Stan. Fran was right, you sure *do* know how to make a fashion statement!"

Stanley's chest swelled with pride. He was wearing a pair of designer cream pants with thin dark chocolate brown stripes. His waistcoat was the reverse, dark chocolate brown with thin cream stripes, and his bow tie matched the pants. He'd bought the outfit only last week from the NextCat Mail Order catalogue, and he was really pleased with them. He pulled out a small, sealed plastic bag from the cupboard, and handed it to Annie. "It's from a Hungarian cat called Laszlo Kiss. His name's on the bag. I've also got one more blue hair from the latest crime scene. My guess is that it'll match the ones that Francesca took over to California."

"Yeah I've brought those samples back so I can make the comparisons. I'll start on the Laszlo Kiss sample straightaway. You said you had two suspects?"

"The other one is being brought in for questioning this morning, so it'll be a simple matter to get a sample from him straightaway. I'll have it sent to the lab as soon as we have it. If you need me, just shout. I'll introduce you to the other members of the team later."

When Jack and Marmaduke arrived at Laszlo's bedsit, on the button of seven o'clock, there was no-one in. They sat in the car and settled down to wait.

"Thank goodness it's Saturday tomorrow," said Jack.

"Shall we play golf, Jackster?

"Only if you promise not to do what you did last time we played!"

"Yeah, that was a disaster. I really got that shot wrong."

"You can say that again."

"I'll never forget the look on the face of that cat in the pay kiosk. He never saw the ball coming did he?"

"I bet he had a sore head for a week." Jack laughed. "So, when are you going to ask Valentina out on a date?"

"Jack, can I ask you a question?"

"Sure."

"Do you think I should try to lose weight?" Marmaduke patted his stomach.

"Too much toast and marmalade, you mean? Couldn't have anything to do with Valentina, could it?" Jack grinned.

Marmaduke blushed. "Well it might help, if I wanted to ask her out on a date."

"Don't tell me you're still undecided. Look, Marmy, you don't need to lose weight, you're fine as you are. But I guess we could both benefit from regular exercise. Why don't we join the Cat-Haven Cat-Gym? It'll be good for us."

"That's a great idea, Jack. Let's do it tomorrow after the golf. Then perhaps I might get up the courage to ask Valentina out."

It was a quarter to nine before Laszlo Kiss finally arrived on foot. Jack and Marmaduke jumped out of their car and raced across the road. They caught up with Laszlo just as he was opening his front door. He turned round when he heard the running footsteps behind him.

"Oh no!" he exclaimed. "Not you two again."

"We'd like to see your passport, sir," said Jack.

"Why?"

"We need to establish that you are in this country legally."

Grudgingly Laszlo entered his room, rummaged

in one of the drawers, and fished out his passport. He handed it to Jack.

"Seems to be in order. I'll just hold onto it for the moment. We need you to come to the station, sir, to answer a few questions."

"What if I don't want to come?"

"We would prefer you to come voluntarily, sir," said Marmaduke.

"But what if I don't want to?"

"I'm afraid we'll have to arrest you, sir."

"Then that's what you'll have to do."

"All right, sir," said Jack. "If that's the way you want it. Marmaduke, read him his rights, and then cuff him."

Marmaduke read Laszlo his rights, and handcuffed his paws behind his back. Then he and Jack frogmarched him across the road. Jack opened the back door of the car, and Marmaduke thrust Laszlo into the back seat and climbed in after him.

Meanwhile Albert Tartpincher had arrived at the station soon after nine and was questioned straightaway by Stanley. The interview lasted no more than twenty minutes, and Stanley knew that he had absolutely no reason to hold him. Perhaps his most telling argument was the very one that Stanley himself had used during the last meeting. He could not have been the mysterious cat checking out the crime scenes, since he would have been recognised by members of staff. And why would he need to use another cat to look over the premises he was already familiar with? All in all, there wasn't a shred of evidence against him. At about the time that Marmaduke was bundling Laszlo Kiss into the cat-police car, Albert Tartpincher walked out of the Cat-Haven Cat-Police station. Nevertheless, Stanley had taken the precaution of obtaining a hair sample, which was sent along to the laboratory for Annie.

"This is Detective Sergeant Stanley Smartpants of Cat-Haven Cat-Police conducting an interview with Mr Laszlo Kiss at 09.56 a.m. on Friday 21st July. Also present is Detective Chief Inspector Derek Dimwit." Stanley turned off the tape machine. "Before we get started Mr Kiss, I gather that you've been pretty uncooperative this morning."

Laszlo Kiss stared straight ahead, and said nothing.

"Let me advise you, Mr Kiss. If you have nothing to hide, you should have no problem answering our questions. The more you cooperate, the easier it will be for you, and the quicker we can finish this." Stanley turned on the tape machine once more.

"Can you please confirm your full name and address."

Laszlo hesitated, but only for a moment. "Laszlo Kiss, 23b Harbour Cottages, Cat-Haven."

"What's your occupation?"

"I'm a cleaner-cat."

"Where do you clean?"

"You know where I clean," he said.

"For the record, Mr Kiss."

"I clean at the Cat-Odeon, the Skating Rink, and the Kitty Kat Ice Cream Parlour."

"Anywhere else?"

"No."

"Are you aware that all three establishments have been robbed in the last two weeks?" asked Derek. As usual Stanley was seated at the table and Derek stood directly behind the suspect.

Laszlo Kiss turned round. "Yes, of course."

"Did you know that a cat answering your description was seen loitering outside two of those locations and outside Cat Diamonds "R" Us, which was also the scene of a robbery?"

"What's that got to do with me?"

Stanley spoke next. "Weren't you that cat Mr Kiss?"

Laszlo Kiss turned back to face Stanley once more. "Certainly not."

"I think you were. We have three witnesses who saw you."

"You couldn't have."

"We'll organise an identity parade shortly," said Derek. "That should help things along."

"It won't do you any good."

"Let's move on. Tell me about your limp?"

Laszlo was obviously puzzled by this question. "What do you mean exactly?"

"When I saw you at the Magyar Palace restaurant on Monday, you limped over to my table."

"And I explained to you that I do sometimes limp after I've been sitting in one position for a long period, like when I'm playing the hurdy-gurdy. It's a condition I was born with. I have a weakness in my left hip. I think I must have inherited it from one of my parents. My brother has it too."

Laszlo bit his lip, as if he'd said too much, and Stanley noticed a flicker of fear in his eyes. He latched on to it straightaway. "Tell me about your brother."

"What do you mean?"

"Where does your brother live? What does he do?"

Laszlo became aggressive. "Mind your own business. My brother is my family, and that's private."

"Nothing is private in this room, Laszlo," said Derek. "And look at me when I'm talking to you. Does your brother live in Cat-Haven?"

Laszlo glanced over his shoulder. "That's for you to find out."

"I take it that's a yes, Laszlo," said Stanley. "If he lived somewhere else I'm sure you would have told us."

"Quite right, Stan," interjected Derek. "You might as well tell us where he lives, Laszlo. We'll find out anyway."

Laszlo said nothing.

Stanley continued with the questioning. "Does your brother limp?"

Laszlo hesitated, obviously unsure how to respond. Stanley guessed that this was an important moment, and waited patiently for Laszlo's reply. "I told you already. He has the same condition that I have. A weakness in the left hip. Of course he limps."

"All the time, or just some of the time?"

"I don't know."

"He's your partner in crime, isn't he?"

"I don't know what you're talking about."

"Or maybe you're *his* partner in crime, Laszlo," said Derek. "Is that how it is?"

Laszlo said nothing.

"I'd like to go back to Monday morning, four days ago," said Stanley. "Where were you at seven o'clock on Monday morning?"

"I was at home in bed."

When Stanley had asked Laszlo the same question in the Magyar Palace, his reply had been hesitant and unconvincing. On this occasion it was neither. But he was unable to prevent the same guilty look from clouding his face. Stanley just knew that he was lying. He nodded briefly to Derek.

Derek noted the gesture and responded as they had planned. "Didn't you tell Sergeant Smartpants that you were at the beach at seven o'clock?"

"No, I didn't."

"What time were you at the beach, then?" said Stanley softly.

Laszlo was clearly upset by the questioning. "I … er … wasn't at the beach. I already told you that."

For the second time Stanley was convinced that Laszlo was lying. "I think we'll take a break now. For the record this part of the interview is terminated at 11.17 a.m." He switched off the tape machine. "We're going for a cup of tea, Laszlo. We'll see you later."

"Can I have a cup of tea?" Laszlo asked.

"Not at this time," replied Stanley. "When you start telling us the truth you can have a cup of tea."

With that Stanley and Derek left the interview room. The key turning in the lock made a loud, clanking sound. When Stanley looked through the peep hole from outside the room, he saw Laszlo wiping the sweat from his brow. "We'll let him stew for an hour," he said to Derek as they climbed the stairs to the first floor.

Stanley had hoped that when they went back into the interview room an hour later, Laszlo would have been softened up a little. But in fact it was the reverse. The delay had somehow stiffened his resolve. They questioned him thoroughly about his cleaning activities at all three premises, but learned nothing of interest. They questioned him about the other three crime scenes, but could not fault him on his answers. They couldn't break him down. Stanley was beginning to lose confidence in his own judgement. Despite this he was still convinced that Laszlo had been at the beach when Harriet had been robbed. And the question mark over Laszlo's brother remained.

He decided to keep Laszlo locked up until Annie had completed her analysis. That at least would prove whether or not he was the thief-cat. But he feared the worst.

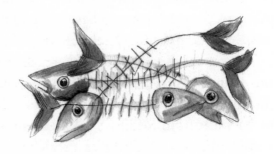

Friday 21st July

It was five thirty before Apple Pie Annie finished her exhaustive DNA analysis. When she walked into Stanley's office her face was grey, and she looked completely exhausted.

"It's bad news I'm afraid, Stan. Neither Albert Tartpincher or Laszlo Kiss is the criminal-cat."

"Is there any room for doubt?"

"No, Stan. The tests are one hundred per cent conclusive."

"Dear oh dear! We're back where we started. We don't have a single suspect. The mayor isn't going to like this."

"Politicians never do, if they think they're gonna lose votes. There's one thing that keeps nagging me though, Stan. The Laszlo Kiss sample has some elements of the DNA present in the samples that were found at the crime scenes."

"What does that mean?"

"I can't be sure about this, Stan. So don't take it as any sort of guarantee."

A shiver of excitement coursed through Stanley's veins. "Come on, Annie, spit it out."

"Well," she continued, "it's possible, just possible you understand, that Laszlo could be related to the criminal-cat."

Stanley jumped out of his chair. "Bingo! It's his brother. He slipped up during the first interview this morning, and admitted that he has a brother. And his brother has a limp, I'm sure of it."

Annie looked puzzled.

"Sorry," said Stanley. "You don't know this, but a blue cat with a limp was spotted hanging around three of the crime scenes a couple of days before the robberies. I saw Laszlo limping at the Hungarian restaurant where he's a musician. He has a hip problem, and so does his brother. He even told me it affected the left hip, so the limp is in the left foot!"

"Have you any idea where to find the brother?"

"No, we couldn't get that information out of him. And it won't be easy. But I just know that Laszlo's got something to do with all this. I'll bet that the criminal-cat is his brother, and that Laszlo knows everything! Annie, you've been a great help. We really appreciate your efforts."

"You're welcome, Stan. To be honest I'm pretty beat. I think I need to go home and get some rest. Do you want me to come in tomorrow?"

"I'm not really sure. Let me give you a call at the apartment tomorrow morning."

Stanley decided on balance that he would not conduct a further interview with Laszlo today. He instructed Jack to go into the interview room and tell Laszlo that he would be staying in one of the cells for the night. There would be more questions for him in the morning. Stanley needed to relax and he sent a text to Peaches.

"Hi Peaches. R u free? Thought we might go 4 a drink. Ill call 4 u if u fancy it"

Peaches replied in less than a minute. *"Luv 2 Stan. C u in 10 mins"*

"You look tired, Stan," was the first thing that Peaches said.

"I am. It's been a tough day. And it started so well."

"Tell me about it if you want to."

"Let's go to the Juicy Grape and I will."

Stanley told her everything, culminating in the disappointment of feeling that the investigation had come to a dead end. There was only one chink of light. Possibly. The outside chance that there might be a relative of Laszlo Kiss that they knew nothing about. Peaches had listened attentively as the story had unfolded. There was a burning question in her mind.

"Stanley," she said. "was that blue Burmese waiter-cat from the Cluck Cluck Diner one of your suspects?"

"What blue Burmese waiter-cat? The only suspect we had at the Cluck Cluck *was* a waiter-cat, but he was a blue Korat, and he was eliminated when it was confirmed that the thief-cat was a blue Burmese."

"No, Stanley, don't you remember? When we arrived at the Cluck Cluck we were shown to our table by a blue Burmese waiter-cat who had a heavy limp."

Stanley was on the point of sipping his glass of wine, but Peaches' revelation almost caused him to drop it on the floor, and his mouth fell open. "Of course," he said, "I remember him now. I think I saw him this morning. I was having breakfast in the Sea View Café, and there was a blue Burmese sitting at another table. At the time I thought that I'd seen him somewhere before, but I couldn't remember when and where. I don't suppose you remember which foot he was limping on?"

"Of course I do. I always remember silly unimportant things like that. It was his left foot that he dragged along the ground."

"Bingo!" Stanley was really excited and leaned forward to kiss Peaches on the cheek. "I think you've just solved the case of the mackerel robberies, Peaches. This is soooo cool! For sure that cat will turn out to be Laszlo's brother, and I bet he's the one we're looking for. I'd put money on it."

"I'd be a bit careful about that if I were you, Stanley. I remember the story you told me about losing your shirt at the roulette table."

Stanley smiled ruefully at the memory. "But not this time, Peaches. I'm sorry, but I have to cut our evening short. I must go to the Cluck Cluck Diner immediately."

"I understand," said Peaches, putting her paw on Stanley's arm.

"You can come with me if you like."

"I'd love to. It'll be special to see the great detective at work!"

"Stop taking the mickey!" Stanley took out his office mobile and scrolled down till he came to Jumping Jack's number. "Hello, Jack, it's Stanley. I need you to drop what you're doing and meet me at the Cluck Cluck Diner in fifteen minutes. We've found our cat. He's Laszlo's brother."

"Jumping Jellybeans! No problem, Sarge. I'll see you there in less than fifteen."

They arrived more or less together. Stanley briefed Jack quickly, and they went in to the restaurant.

Larry Cluck Cluck saw them as soon as they walked in, and he waddled over towards them. "What do you want?" he said rudely.

"You have a blue Burmese waiter-cat with a pronounced limp. Is he working tonight?"

"I presume you mean Hungaro."

"Bingo!" said Stanley under his breath. "That'll be him. Is he on tonight?"

Larry Cluck Cluck checked his watch. "He should be here any time now."

"We'll wait."

Larry Cluck Cluck looked daggers at Peaches. "I would offer you something, but I know it wouldn't be high class enough for you."

Peaches bit her tongue. She would have loved to sock it to this disagreeable cat! But she knew that this was a very important moment for Stanley. It would be wrong to get involved in a slanging match with Larry Cluck Cluck.

Stanley, Jack and Peaches sat down at the table nearest the door. They didn't have to wait long before a blue Burmese limped into the restaurant. It was the same cat Stanley had seen in the Sea View Café two days ago. Both he and Jack were on their feet in a flash.

"Good evening, sir," said Stanley flipping open his warrant card. "I'm Detective Sergeant Stanley Smartpants of the Cat-Haven Cat-Police. And this is my colleague, Detective Cat-Constable Jumping Jack. We'd like a few words with you."

The Burmese stared at them arrogantly. "What do you want?"

"First of all we'd like you to confirm your name."

"They call me Hungaro."

"We need your real name, sir."

"Hungaro is good enough."

"Don't play games with us. We know that your surname is Kiss, but we'd like your first name."

The Burmese was clearly shaken by this, and the arrogant confidence of a moment ago evaporated. "Sandor," he said simply.

"We'd like you to accompany us to the station, Mr Kiss. We have some questions we'd like to ask you."

"About what?"

"I think you know that, Mr Kiss. It's about what the Cat-Haven Chronicle calls the mackerel robberies." Stanley thought that he detected a resigned look on the face of Sandor Kiss. It had certainly changed to a pale shade of blue.

"I suppose I don't have a choice, do I?"

Stanley gave the keys to Jack's car to Peaches so that she could drive home, and arranged to call her after they had finished with the Burmese.

They took Sandor Kiss into Interview Room Two, the one next to Interview Room One, where they had interviewed Laszlo earlier. Stanley asked Cheerful Charlie to bring Laszlo up from the cells, and put him back in Interview Room One. It was Laszlo they spoke to first.

Jack turned on the tape machine, and recorded the time and date details. "We have something to show you, Laszlo."

Stanley reached under the desk and pressed the button concealed there. The panel in the wall slid silently back. The two-way mirror revealed the next room. Sandor Kiss was sitting at the desk, gazing into space.

A startled expression crossed Laszlo's face, and he began to shake.

"A bit of a surprise for you, Laszlo?" said Stanley.

Laszlo said nothing, but Stanley could almost hear his brain working overtime. Wondering what to do. He was opening and closing his claws in obvious frustration. Suddenly his resolve failed him. "I told him it was a stupid thing to do," he whispered.

"What was stupid, Laszlo?" said Stanley. He knew that this was a crucial moment, and that as long as he handled the situation competently, Laszlo would tell them everything they wanted to know.

"I told him it was a stupid idea to steal the mackerel from the female fishercat."

"On the beach? On Monday morning?"

"Yes." Laszlo's voice was strained, resigned.

"Tell us exactly what happened."

Laszlo let out a great sigh before continuing. "He wanted me to go with him, to act as a lookout. To protect his back. I told him that if he wanted more mackerel, he could easily buy them from the fish market. But he said there wouldn't be any pleasure in buying them. That it would be a thrill to steal them."

"Why did he want to steal some mackerel?" probed Stanley gently.

"Because the original mackerel he'd stolen from the Cluck Cluck Diner had all been used."

"These original mackerel, were they left at the scene of the robberies that have hit Cat-Haven in the last two weeks?"

Laszlo nodded his head sadly. "Yes."

With Laszlo's statement in their pockets, it did not take long to persuade Sandor to come clean. Within a couple of hours he had signed a full confession, admitting the thefts at all six crime scenes. It was Jack who asked him why he had deposited the skeleton of a mackerel at every one of them.

"The first one, at that old granny's house, was a mistake. I'd been eating the mackerel just before I broke into her house. After I'd pocketed the cash, I thought I heard a noise. I panicked, and ran off, leaving the mackerel behind. I completely forgot that I'd taken it out of my mouth in order to jump up onto the wardrobe. After that it just appealed to my sense of humour to leave a dead mackerel as my 'calling card'. And once it made the front page of the Cat-Haven Chronicle, and they called it the mackerel robberies, I felt committed to carry on with it." Sandor forced a wan smile.

"We have several witnesses to the fact that a Blue Burmese was seen loitering outside three of the crime scenes," said Stanley. "At Cat Diamonds "R" Us, the Skating Rink, and the Kitty Kat Ice Cream Parlour. "Was that you or Laszlo?"

The unexpectedness of the question flummoxed Sandor Kiss. Stanley waited, aware that Sandor was weighing up his options.

"Of course it was me," said Sandor. "My brother has nothing to do with this."

"As we've already said to you," said Stanley, "it was Laszlo who told us about you."

"He had nothing to do with any of the robberies."

"It was Laszlo who gave you the inside information on the premises where he worked as a cleaner, wasn't it?"

"No, he didn't."

Stanley and Jack were unable to get Sandor to admit that Laszlo had played any part in the crimes. And although Stanley was convinced that he had been more than just a lookout when Harriet Fishnet had been robbed, they had no choice but to release him.

"Disappointing that we couldn't nail Laszlo," said Stanley, but that was a good night's work, Jack. It's a good feeling to have cracked the case of the mackerel robberies. Thanks for coming out at such short notice."

"No problem, Sarge. It was great to be in at the end of it."

"I think we'll have our celebration dinner tomorrow evening, Jack. Can you ask Charlie if he can contact every cat on the team, and tell them we're going to have a party tomorrow evening. As usual we'll go to the Juicy Grape Wine Bar. Say eight o'clock. Tell him I'll call the Chief. I think he'd like to hear the news from me personally."

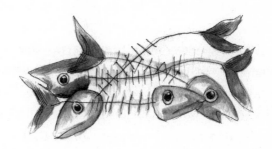

Saturday 22nd July – midday

S tanley spent the morning completing the paperwork on the mackerel robberies. He had not been in the mood for it last night. Instead, he had gone for a quiet, relaxing drink with Peaches. Finally the paperwork was done, and he sat back in his chair. Another case solved, he thought to himself with satisfaction. But in the endless fight against cat-crime, he knew that he could never rest on his laurels. The next big case was already on his desk. However, that was in the future. For now, it was time for their traditional celebration dinner after cracking a big case. It would be wild! As usual.

Saturday 22nd July – 8.00 p.m.

Almost everyone was there. The only notable exception was Cheerful Charlie. As usual, he volunteered to man the station. Stanley paid for these celebrations out of his own pocket, and no expense was spared. Some of the cadet-cats, and of course Apple Pie Annie, had no idea what they were in for. And nobody was about to tell them!

They had hired the private room at the Juicy Grape Wine Bar, which meant that they wouldn't have to worry about disapproving looks from members of the cat-public. Twenty cats sat round a huge, elongated 'H' shaped table.

They had a fantastic five course meal, and naturally the drinks flowed freely. There was plenty of wine with dinner, although the younger cadet-cats had to make do with soft drinks such as Cat-Cola and Six-Up. Formality was out of the window. It was Stanley's wish that on these occasions everyone was equal. There were no bosses, no titles, no formality of any kind. Only cat-colleagues. When Stanley had started this tradition, this had been the first and only rule. At first, Chief Inspector Dimwit had not been in favour of it. He felt that it would encourage a lack of respect amongst the younger cats. Stanley's view was the complete opposite. He felt that it was a great exercise in cat-team bonding. When Stanley gave Derek a stark choice: be part of it on my terms, or don't bother to come, Derek gave in.

Stanley pinged his glass with a spoon, and all his cats fell silent. He got to his feet, and walked round to the back of his chair. He was wearing his newest and most expensive smart pants. They were a shiny black with broad silver stripes and fashionable turn ups, and covered much of his shiny, black leather shoes. He was very proud of them. And he was wearing a frilly, long sleeved purple silk shirt and a black and silver striped bow tie. He looked and felt a million dollars!

"To celebrate the successful conclusion to the mackerel robberies case," he began, "I've written a special poem. Here it is.

> *There once was a cat that we called Klepto Klaws*
> *And he had it is true a number of flaws.*
> *He took on a neckless,*
> *Which proved to be reckless.*
> *And now there's no question of bail,*
> *Old Klepto is straight off to jail.*
> *As for Hungaro, the multiple thief,*
> *He had it is plain a foolish belief.*
> *With mackerel bones he picked clean*
> *And disguised by a fancy cuisine,*
> *He hoped and he prayed that he would us confuse,*
> *Unaware that for us there were plenty of clues.*
> *Although it is true that he had a head start*
> *He ran out of luck*
> *At the Diner Cluck Cluck.*
> *'Cos we gave it our soul and we gave it our heart,*
> *And for criminal-cats we're much much too smart!"*

****

The rapturous applause and joyous laughter that followed, made Stanley feel like two million dollars! It was plain that every cat in the room loved his 'end of case' poem. The mood of everyone was very relaxed. Many of the cats took off their shoes, including Stanley.

It was time for the games and competitions to begin. The purpose of the evening was FUN – FUN – FUN! And everyone joined in. There was Pass the Parcel with a variety of quirky prizes, charades, pin the tail on the mackerel, apple bobbing, and much more.

One tradition that had been established early on during the first of these celebrations was the bread throwing competition. Not just any bread throwing, you understand. That would have been tiresome. This was organised bread throwing, which continued throughout the evening. Stanley had a bell in front of him, which was the most important item in the room, since it governed all the organised games. One ring of the bell signalled bread throwing. Three cats stood up, and each threw a piece of bread in turn. The bread could be thrown at any cat of the thrower's choice. Inevitably, Derek and Stanley were the main victims. Points were awarded for a direct hit, extra points for a hit flush on the nose or between the eyes. Stanley made the decisions and Studious Stephen kept the running scores.

Throughout the course of the evening each cat took a total of six throws. The prize was awarded to the cat with the lowest score, in other words the cat who had the most failures at hitting the intended target. The prize was one that no cat wanted to win.

The very last throw of the competition fell to Apple Pie Annie. She paused dramatically, and dunked her piece of bread in the water jug for several seconds. Then she squeezed it in her paw, looking round the table, pretending that she was trying to decide which cat to throw it at. After a while she hurled it at Stanley, and it caught him smack in the kisser! Instead of just bouncing off his face, as a piece of dry bread would have done, the soggy missile had turned into a lumpy, squidgy, squelchy, squishy mess, and it clung to his mouth and chin. He was forced to scrape it off with his paw, and dry his face with a napkin. Howls of laughter greeted this episode, and Annie grinned hugely.

"How did that grab you, Stan?" she said.

Stanley laughed. "It was pretty good, Annie. Nobody's going to beat that. I'll just have to give you the maximum ten points."

"Yes, but was it better than a slap in the eye with a wet fish, Stan?" said Jack with a cheeky grin on his face.

Both Jack and Annie looked pleased with

themselves, and smiled at the other cats. Marmaduke noted the expression on Stanley's face, and nudged Jack in the ribs. "This isn't over yet, Jackster," he whispered behind his paw.

"That's the end of the bread competition," said Stanley. "Stephen can you give us the scores." Those cats who had been to a celebration dinner before, knew that the prize would go to the cat with the lowest score. And no cat wanted to win this particular prize. Jack had told Cynthia what to expect, and she looked on now with mounting apprehension. She knew that she had made a mess of her throws, and that she had a low score. Vincent was also worried. He too had failed to achieve many points. His nerves got the better of him and he stood up.

"Sorry, Sarge, I mean Stanley, but I'm afraid I think that I need to go for a poo. I'm not sure, but I think so."

Stanley nodded. Jack and Marmaduke poked each other in the ribs. Tammy and Pamela could hardly contain themselves and giggled noisily. Greta smiled at Annie, who was beginning to sense that something unpleasant was about to happen. Tammy and Pamela exchanged knowing looks, happy in the knowledge that they were safe. Derek Dimwit looked slightly uncomfortable. He often thought in circumstances such as these that he was lucky to be a short-haired moggie, for he found it so difficult to let his hair down.

Vincent ran towards the door and opened it wide. He stood in the doorway, unable to make up his mind whether to go or to stay.

"Make your mind up, Vinnie," shouted Jack. "Do you want to hear a joke about going for a poo while you're deciding, Vinnie?"

"Oh, yes please Jack," squeaked Cynthia.

"Well, I don't know one," said Jack. "Ha! Ha! Ha!"

"I don't like to complain about the door being open, Vinnie," said Greta, "but ….."

"Well don't then," said Marmaduke grinning at Jack.

"Hurry up and close that door, Vinnie," said Derek. "One way or another. We don't want the cat-public staring at us."

Vinnie still couldn't make up his mind. Pamela got up from her chair and coaxed him back to the table.

Studious Stephen looked miserable. He had failed to hit a single target, and since he was the cat keeping score, he knew that he was in last place, and was destined to receive the prize. He read out the scores in reverse order.

"This is soooo cool," said Stanley. "I'm going to make a change to the rules, and give the prize to the cat with the highest score, rather than the lowest. That's you, Annie, with squintillions of points."

Stephen's face was a picture of happiness.

"Hear, hear," said Jack, clapping his paws excitedly. "Give her the prize now, Stan."

There was laughter around the table, and Annie looked on suspiciously. She was beginning to think that she might just regret what she had done. Stanley smiled crookedly, and picked up the phone on the table. The voice of a disembodied cat answered.

"Send in the bread pudding please," was all Stanley said.

Moments later a waitress-cat appeared, carrying a huge bowl of ...... well .... words cannot describe the dish that was put in front of Annie. It looked absolutely disgusting, a dirty brown mess of mulch! All those cats who knew what was coming next sat forward expectantly, their eyes shining with delight.

"Come on, Stan," shouted Marmaduke. "It's time for the 'Bread Poem'!"

Stanley stood up. All the cats, except for the new recruits and Apple Pie Annie of course, knew Stanley's famous 'bread poem'. They knew that the prize was normally given to the cat with the lowest score. But since Stanley had stood the rules on their head, they wondered if he would introduce a variation in the poem this time round. They were not to be disappointed. Stanley looked pointedly at Annie as he began to speak.

> *"If you cannot hit a cat between the eyes,*
> *You may be the one to win our special prize.*

For you, dear Annie, I've had to change the rule,
Because, dear Annie, you made me look a fool!
The dish that you are now to eat,
Will be for you a magic treat.
A dish that's made of bread and cream and custard,
And just for fun some ketchup and some mustard!"

"Yuck!" cried Tammy and Pamela in unison.

There was much laughter, hooting and hollering, and paws banging the table in a rhythmic beat, as the cats began to chant:

"Eat! Eat! Eat! .... Eat! Eat! Eat!"

Annie closed her eyes and spooned a portion into her mouth. It was as vile as it looked, and the expression on her face was priceless. Every cat cheered and clapped:

"Eat! Eat! Eat! .... Eat! Eat! Eat!"

Even though she hated every mouthful, Annie pressed on, determined to uphold the honour of California, and the USA, determined not to let the Brits defeat her. When she was about half way through the 'magic treat', the cats began to applaud and shout out:

"Well done Annie!"

"You're a star!"

"What a sport!"

"Super Annie!"

Annie smiled to herself, and guessed that she had eaten enough.

"How did *that* grab you, Annie?" said a laughing Stanley.

"It was cool, Stan. Nobody's gonna beat that. Wow that sucked!"

Stanley excused himself, and set off towards the toilet, leaving his shoes where they were under the table. The excitement of the last few minutes had died down, and all the cats of the Cat-Haven Cat-Police assumed that the festivities were at an end. But not so! Annie had one more trick up her sleeve.

The moment that Stanley left the room, she leapt up from the table and picked up his shoes. Furiously she shovelled what remained of the 'magic treat' into them. There was a bottle of salad cream on the table, and she emptied this into the mixture for good measure, and half a glass of left over red wine. She managed to fill both shoes up to the brim. Then she put them back under the table, exactly where they had been.

Every cat in the room watched in fascination, and growing excitement. At last Stanley returned. He saw the smiles and excited faces of his cat-colleagues, and he felt the surge of excitement that jumped up to meet him as he padded back to the table. Foolishly he assumed that they were all still enjoying the final moments of the bread competition. Not for one moment did he imagine what was to follow.

"Time to go, I guess," he said. "It's been a really special night."

"Even more special than you think," shouted out Jack.

Riotous laughter greeted Jack's comment, but Stanley did not twig that anything was amiss. As he blindly placed his feet into his shoes, his first reaction was surprise at the wall of sound that attacked him. Every single cat, including Derek Dimwit, burst out laughing, and started to clap. The noise was deafening. As his feet squelched into the gooey, soggy mess in his shoes, a look of absolute horror spread across his face. He looked down to see the turn-ups of his precious black and silver striped trousers covered in the dirty brown 'bread pudding' mixture.

Annie looked him directly in the eyes, and said with a perfectly straight face, "How did *that* grab *you*, Stan?"

THE END

Now read the first chapter of Alexander Martin's next book in the Stanley Smartpants series,

Stanley Smartpants and the Harbour Mystery

To be published in 2012, and available online at
www.stanleysmartpants.co.uk

Chapter 1

Wednesday 7th December

S tanley stood in the doorway gazing at his boss, shaking his head in disbelief. It was shortly after half past nine in the morning, and Chief Inspector Derek Dimwit of the Cat-Haven Cat-Police was fast asleep. His screechy, scratchy, squeaky snoring caused Stanley to wonder if he might be ill. But it had a curious and repetitive sing-song rhythm, and sounded like an express train clattering through a railway station at top speed.

Stanley coughed, but there was no response. He coughed again, but this time louder. "Ahem! Ahem!"

At last Derek opened one eye and looked at Stanley suspiciously.

"There's been a robbery on a yacht moored in Brixcat Harbour, Chief," said Stanley.

"It doesn't sound very important. Tell me about it later, Stan." Derek closed his unblinking eye and snuggled deeper into the comfort of his padded leather chair.

"We can't let the grass grow under our paws on this one, Chief. The yacht belongs to the squintillionaire politician-cat, Sir Lancelot Smiles-a-Lot."

"I hear what you say, Stan, but you should never wake a cat when he's in the middle of a catnap," said Derek sleepily, his eyes still tight shut.

Detective Sergeant Stanley Smartpants was not to be put off so easily. "Your cousin, the Mayor, won't be pleased if we don't deal with this quickly."

Before Stanley could say any more, a cat who was similar in colour to a jar of Seville orange marmalade rushed into Derek's office, two slices of toast and marmalade clutched in his paws. "It's an emergency, Chief," he spluttered. "Tammy's fallen into the chocolate pudding!"

At the mention of chocolate pudding Derek Dimwit was instantly awake and alert. "What chocolate pudding?" he said, licking his whiskers in anticipation.

"Chocolate pudding!" exclaimed Stanley. "That is sooooo cool!" His face broke into a beaming smile, and he waggled his chocolate brown ears.

Cat-Constable Marmalade Marmaduke, a Red Tabby Shorthair, took a bite out of both slices of toast and marmalade at virtually the same time. Oodles and oodles of crumbs from his mouth fell onto the carpet.

Derek was annoyed. "You shouldn't waltz into my office eating toast, Marmaduke. You should show me more respect. And you should have knocked."

Marmaduke shrugged his shoulders. With his mouth

still full of toast he said, "I couldn't, Chief. My paws were unavailable." Pointedly he looked at his paws, still clutching his toast. "Anyway they were sticky."

"F-f-f-f-f-forget it, Marmaduke," stammered Derek. "What's this about a chocolate pudding? Why didn't one of you cats come and wake me? You know how much I love chocolate pudding!"

"Me too, Chief," said Marmaduke. "I'm reeeally, reeeally, reeeally hungry!"

"Let's go and sort this out," said Stanley. He hitched up his colourful trousers and strode out of Derek's office.

As he opened the door of the Crime Room, Stanley was greeted by an incredible scene. Cat-Constable Tammy Tickletummy, a gorgeous Seal Point Siamese, who was normally easy to recognise on account of her soft white coat, was standing on top of the conference table, dripping chocolate, and looking as miserable as a wet weekend in winter. She was covered from whisker to paw in Catbury's Dairy Milk cat-chocolate pudding, and no cat could have guessed the colour of her fur.

Cat-Constable Jumping Jack was winding himself up to jump onto the table. He had announced that he was going to lick Tammy to pieces, and was being egged on by the female cadet-cats. Just as Jack leapt onto the table, Derek came marching into the room. And the moment he saw the chaotic scene in front of him his plain, black and white face turned purple. "What are you cats doing?" he demanded.

But no-one was listening.

"Why don't we have a chocolate dance," said Marmaduke. "Pamela, switch on Tammy's iPod Shuffle.

Let's have some music."

"Now look here c-c-c-c-cats," said Derek. "This is unacceptable b-b-b-b-behaviour." Derek had an unfortunate habit of stammering when he was flustered.

"It's our chocolate break, Chief," said Jack, tongue in cheek. "Tammy will tell you, we can do what we like during our breaks."

Tammy was usually quick to point out their cat-rights in the work place, but she still looked miserable and said nothing.

Jack jumped up onto the table and pretended to trip over his own feet. He was an American Wirehair, a breed of cat that has frizzy fur. In Jack's case it was so spiky it looked as if he had had an electric shock! He fell into Tammy's arms. "Oops!" he said, "sorry Tammy." He didn't look very sorry, and took the opportunity to open his mouth as wide as possible. His tongue darted in and out with the speed of Jerry trying to escape from Tom, and with each dart of his tongue he licked as much chocolate as he could from Tammy's fur.

The situation was getting out of hand, and Stanley took charge. Conveniently he had a spoon in his trouser pocket, a spoon that was soon to be put to serious chocolate use! He banged it several times on the edge of a desk.

Every cat in the Crime Room knew that Stanley was about to deliver one of his famous poems, and they all fell silent.

"A choc'late pudding is for cats a treat,
And into it to fall is not so neat.
Why Tammy fell into the pud we cannot guess,

IV

A shower is what she needs, a lick would make a mess.

Nor do we know why Jack would like to lick her clean.

'Cos Jack, my friend, you do not know where else she's been!"

There was a lot of noisy laughter and clapping from those cats who were in the room. Stanley's poems always went down well.

Tammy was a bit put out. "You shouldn't be making a joke at my expense, Sergeant. It's against my cat-rights in the work place. And it's not fair!"

"Come on Tammy," said Marmaduke, "lighten up."

Tammy glowered at Marmaduke. "I thought you would have taken my side, Marmy."

"I *am* taking your side, Tammy. It's not so serious, now is it?"

Before Tammy could reply Playful Pamela jumped in. "Come on, Tammy, I'll take you to the showers. The Sarge is right, you need to get cleaned up."

Stanley looked round for Soppy Cynthia, but couldn't see her anywhere. It was she who had taken the telephone call reporting the robbery. "Where's Cynthia gone?"

"I'm here, Sarge," she said from the far corner of the Crime Room. Cadet-Cat Soppy Cynthia was an unusual breed of cat, a Red Spotted Tabby Munchkin, with short legs and a short tail. And she looked unusual too. When she sat up on her haunches with her paws off the ground, as she did now, she looked more like a squirrel than a cat!

"Cynthia, just refresh my memory about the telephone call you took."

"What telephone call?" said Cynthia. She had a puzzled

look on her face.

Stanley sighed inwardly. "You said the Harbour Master-cat from Brixcat Harbour called."

"Oh, yes," said Cynthia, blushing heavily. "Silly me! I was so interested in the chocolate pudding that I almost forgot about it."

"So, what did the Harbour Master-cat say?" asked Stanley.

"He said that Sir Lancelot Smiles-a-Lot has suffered a serious robbery. The safe on his boat has been broken into, and loads of jewellery and cash has been stolen."

"Is that all?"

"Isn't that enough, Sarge," interrupted Jack, winking at Marmaduke, "having cash and jewellery stolen?"

Stanley turned towards Jack, and raised a disapproving eyebrow. "Did he say anything else, Cynthia?"

"He also said he knows who stole it all," said Cynthia.

"Who was it?" asked Stanley.

"He didn't say."

"Didn't you ask him, Cynthia?"

"No," said Cynthia, her face reddening. "I was so excited that I forgot to ask him."

"Shall I ring him back and find out, Sarge?" asked Jack.

Derek butted in without thinking. "No, don't worry Jack, Stanley and I are on our way there now. After we've had some chocolate pudding, of course! We'll ask him ourselves. It's good to know that the crime is already solved. I wonder who did it?"